Sugar Kisses

3:AM Kisses Book 3

D1520763

ADDISON MOORE

Edited by: Sarah Freese
Cover design by: Regina Wamba of www.MaeIDesign.com
Interior design and formatting by: Gaffey Media

Books by Addison Moore:

Ephemeral (The Countenance Trilogy 1)
Evanescent (The Countenance Trilogy 2)
Entropy (The Countenance Trilogy 3)
Ethereal Knights (Celestra Knights)

Prologue

Roxy

Three things you should know about me.

I hate people.

I'm pretty much invisible to my parents, except when my mother tries to control me.

And the only light in my life, my grandmother, passed away when I was twelve.

I suppose if you reverse the order, it can explain a lot of psychological bullshit that I'm not about to delve into, mostly because I'm allergic to psychological bullshit. I'm all about carving my own path in life, and that just so happens to be through other people's stomachs. I bake. And because ovens are not your standard dorm-issued appliance at Whitney Briggs University, I also now room with a sexual predator in the making, WB's own manwhore, Cole Brighton.

ADDISON MOORE

He takes a step toward me with an animalistic glint in his eye.

His lips twitch with a smile. He comes in close, then closer... His eyes round out as he comes in for the kill. There's a boyishness about him that I find unmistakably attractive, and I wish I didn't. I wish I could say I was immune to all of Cole Brighton's wicked ways, but God knows I'm weak and about to fold. Not to mention the fact that one naked selfie of the two of us tangled up in each other's arms would be a great congratulations-on-your-new-relationship gift to send my ex-boyfriend.

"I think I'm going to kiss you," he whispers right over my lips.

"Relax." I press a hand to his chest and push him away. "I'm not going to kiss you back."

"Why the hell not?" His brows arch so far up into his forehead they almost reach his hairline. Cole looks genuinely stumped by this development.

"Because you like the ladies, remember? And you should probably be neutered." I start in on frosting the cupcakes he christened with an indecent nickname because, God knows, I don't have time to properly explain the order of the universe to Cole *and* get my *little pink tits* frosted in time. "Besides, I'm not interested in a hookup. That's not what I'm about."

Cole picks my chin up gently with his finger and makes me drink down his stare. "Maybe that's not what I'm

6

about anymore either." I watch as he snatches his keys and heads for the door. "Look, I really believe there's a nice person living under that layer of sarcasm." He pauses like he wants to say more but has decided to swallow down his words instead. "I'll be at the gym. Call me if you need a ride to wherever it is you're going." He pauses for a moment. "I promise you, the whole world isn't out to get you, Rox. A lot of people would love to help if you just open up and let them in." And with that he walks out the door.

Let them in?

I bet he'd like for me to *open up* and let him *in*.

I beat the shit out of the butter in an attempt to soften it, but, much like my heart, it's a lost cause. It needs to melt slowly, sort of the way Cole is melting me slowly.

But it'll be a cold day in hell when I let Cole Brighton bring my hormones to a rolling boil.

And, unfortunately, something tells me the weather forecast in hell is about to get a little frigid.

1

Lips Like Sugar

Roxy

You know that feeling you get when you're in the middle of a one-night stand, and the headboard thrashes into the wall, over and over, like a thousand demons begging to burst from the gates of hell?

Yeah, neither do I.

I twist in my bed and stomp my stilettos into my roommate's adjoining wall, but their wild fucking spree continues undaunted.

Cole Brighton is my new cellmate, and he's been persona non grata since I moved in a couple of days ago. He's been too busy entertaining the ladies, moaning into all hours of the night as if he were having a genuine religious experience while worshiping at the altar of coed vagina.

My phone buzzes softly, and I pluck it off the bed. I've already ignored two texts from my mother. In all fairness, Christmas was a few days ago, and I've paid my familial dues for the year. It's not that I don't love my mother, it's just that hanging out with her for even a limited amount of time is the equivalent of drinking a cup full of vinegar— doable and yet regrettable. She hinted over the holidays that it was high time she molded me into an acceptable socialite, and it took everything in me not to hurl all over her pointy toed Prada's. But it's not Mom, it's a text from Laney.

At the door. You in there?

I spring up and head over. To my surprise, my sweet, older brother is right by Laney's side. Now that they're together again, they're practically inseparable. True love will do that to people, glue them at the hip—not that I would know. For me true love proved to be an apparition straight from hell, and I'm not too sorry I chased it away.

"I was getting worried." Ryder offers a half-hearted hug as he makes his way inside. We have the same dark hair, our father's serious eyes, and drive to succeed in business—only Ryder sort of *is* succeeding in business, whereas I'm floundering, about to turn belly up. But, in order to rectify that, I blanketed campus this afternoon with a crap ton of flyers advertising my new upstart, Roxy's Cupcake Catering. *There's nothing too wild or difficult we can't do!* Only the *we* is actually just me, and I'm sort of determined to keep it that way because, for one, I hate people. Not all people, just most people. The two currently gawking around the apartment happened to be off my shit list, for now—although, I'm not above demoting. Life's been pretty crappy overall. My mother is a hard ass, so maybe that's where I get the bad attitude. However, she never had an asshole shit on her heart, so she couldn't properly channel her feelings of hatred and rage toward mankind like I can. Aiden Ryerson, my boyfriend of three years, is the aforementioned asshole who defecated over my beating heart, and I'd like to return the favor by way of tearing out his, but I'm not in the mood for prison—yet.

"How's the kitchen?" Laney asks, inspecting the tiny domesticated square that consists of a four burner electric stove and microwave. I've stacked my flattened pastry boxes in the corner and spread out my mixing bowls and baking utensils because I like to see them laid out like art.

"Compared to the Easy Bake?" I smirk at the sight. "It's an improvement."

I bake. That's how I handle all the bullshit life likes to sling my way thanks to the coping skill passed down from my grandmother. I glance up at her wooden spoon hanging from a ribbon on the wall. It's my homage to her sweet, butter-loving soul. I can't wait to hang that wooden spoon up in my very first storefront, of course, that's before I franchise the business and proliferate the planet with my tasty treats on my way to world domination. If there's one thing my father taught me, it's go big or go home. He might have a heart of steel, but he's a got a bank account full of cash that testifies to his business know-how, and, believe you me, I've been taking notes.

"Anyway"—I flail my arms around the tiny quarters—"I'm more than happy to have a kitchen. And if listening to Cole roar out sexual commands for the next few months is what it takes to have one, then I say bring on the sex toys because this kinky cooking party is just getting started."

Ryder chokes on his next breath.

"Knock, knock!" Baya pokes her head through the door before stepping inside. "Just got back from dropping my mom off at the airport and wanted to see how you're settling in." She bops over and offers a strangulating group hug to both me and Laney. Baya is cute both inside and out. She's bubbly as all hell, which usually makes me want to throat punch puppies, but I've given Baya a pass because she's genuinely a nice person.

"Everything's fine. I've already unpacked and taken over what little of the bathroom counter there was, officially claiming female dominance over your brother." True story. I planted my Tampax right next to his razor. It was my way of saying, *hello, I have a vagina that your penis will never invade. I bleed once a month, and if you don't stay out of my way, chances are, you will, too.*

Baya belts out a laugh. "I knew I liked you."

"Hey, what's this?" Ryder calls from the far end of the living room, and we head on over.

He runs his finger across rows and rows of scratches, etched along the door jam in groups of five with slashes through them.

"Tally marks." Baya makes a face. "That's me." She points to the bottom where there's a line enwreathed with a heart.

"Ah, yes"—Laney leans in as if she were reading fine text—"the infamous, notches for crotches."

"This is Bryson's side." Baya shakes her head. "Not his finest hour." She points to the back wall, and we spin to find another, far more elaborate, series of chicken scratch. "That's Cole's slut meter."

The walls thunder around us. A groan escapes from under Cole's bedroom door as if it were a plea for help, then panting—lots and lots of cataclysmic panting. Clearly an orgasm of nuclear proportions is on the horizon.

"What the fuck?" Ryder looks as if he's ready to help free the captives.

"That's exactly what's going on." Laney pulls him back.

"No." He shakes his head, the rage brewing in his eyes as if it were me being defiled in there. "Are you serious?" He shoots those baby blues back to the scoreboard. "This is some kind of *fuck*-o-meter?" He straightens as if he were struck with a cattle prod. "Get your stuff, Rox, there's no way I'm letting you stay."

"He's got an electric stove," I fire back. "It'll be a cold day in hell when you drag me back to that kitchenless dorm."

"I've got a Viking range that puts out fifteen thousand BTU's and a double convection oven. Pack your shit, Roxy. You're coming to my place."

Laney pinches her lips. I'm pretty sure she doesn't want me hanging around right after they've just moved in together. I'll be a third wheel on their faux-honeymoon. And, believe me, I'd much rather listen to *Baya's* brother heaving himself into a sexual oblivion than my own.

"Forget it. I like being close to campus." True story. Whitney Briggs is right across the street, and I hate to break it to my brother, but one of us doesn't actually own a car, and with no job it would make it far less fuel-efficient to drive if I did.

A sharp groan vibrates through my new roommate's door.

"And on that note..." Baya pivots on her heels. "See you guys at the Black Bear tonight. We have one of the biggest shows of the year planned."

"What's up at the Black Bear?" It's a bar down the street that Baya's boyfriend owns—or at least his family does. Both Laney and Baya work there part time.

"LeAnn Cleo is going on, that's what." Her eyes round out as if Christmas were about to happen all over again.

"LeAnn Cleo!" Laney jumps, and her boobs nearly knock her out in the process. Obviously a bra was optional today.

"Who's that?" Ryder looks unimpressed, as he should.

I groan. "Some pop slash country sensation that sings to preteen girls at shopping malls. Her fifteen minutes were up five years ago, and it looks like no one got the memo."

"Oh, stop." Laney averts her eyes. "Her newest album went double platinum in November, and she's got every major arena sold out for her summer concert tour." She turns to Ryder. "She's decided to complete her education right here at Whitney Briggs while pursuing her career. She was like a ghost on campus last fall because she was trying to keep things low key, but the media got wind of it, and now she's a loud and proud part of the WB student body."

"Aiden had a class with her." I don't know why I brought him up other than the fact I can't seem to get him out of my fucking mind. I hate that I let him burrow in so deep, take root, and continue to kill me long after he walked out on me. I let Laney and Baya think it was a mutual decision, but a part of me would have taken him back if he wanted to keep using me like a doormat. I hate that stupid part of me. But, now that we've had some clearance of a few measly weeks, I can see that I'm better off without the village idiot hanging on like some unwanted appendage. I just need to figure out how to let my heart in on this news.

The room grows decidedly silent save for some residual giggling taking place in Cole's bedroom. I've been here several days and have yet to see him in the flesh. Suffice it to say his flesh has been quite in demand. I counted three different girls leaving at about two in the morning. They were all tiny, fake blondes with boobs, nails, and hair extensions all freshly purchased from the local Build-A-Slut Workshop. I never did see the skank Aiden left me for, but I'm pretty sure he, like all males, has an affinity for stock bimbos.

Laney lands an arm over my shoulders. "Let's get you to the Black Bear tonight and have some fun." Her warm perfume wraps around me like a bubble, and I want to stay right here in her arms and trash men, but Ryder is here. He's about the only male I wouldn't trash outside of Bryson.

"For sure!" Baya jumps up and down. "You never know, you might find the man of your dreams and fall madly in love."

I snarl at the idea.

I don't believe in fun.

I don't believe in the man of my dreams, and, for sure, I don't believe in that four-letter word—*love*.

I glance up at the fuck-'em-and-leave-'em scoreboard and surmise my new roommate feels the exact same way.

Who knows, we might just get along better than I thought.

ᎶᏅᏯ

The Black Bear Saloon is filled with the half-baked student body from a trio of universities nearby. Bryson Edwards and his brother Holt run this hangover hovel. They card everyone in the place, but I know for a fact half of the inebriated coeds bopping around with their silicon milk jugs are underage. That's Aiden's side business, fake IDs. I should turn him in to the feds and watch him fry in the electric chair, better yet, see how far his pretty boy looks get him in prison. I'm betting some man named "Bubba" could get a lot of bartering done by pimping Aiden out as his bitch.

The bar holds the heady scent of liquor and perfume, an intoxicating combo all on its own. Now and again a guy walks by wearing too much cologne, and every ounce of estrogen in me stretches in his direction.

I spot Melanie Harrison in the back with a bunch of her sorority sisters. Melanie is my only real competitor for the Sticky Quickie baking competition coming up in February. She specializes in orgasmic confections and has been wowing everyone on campus with her Ecstasy Delights.

I growl at her before turning around.

"Isn't this great?" Baya orbits around me like a hummingbird, going on and on about this and that, but I can't seem to keep track of her exuberance. My eyes have had the misfortune of fixating on an all-too-familiar dumbass in a pair of chinos with his arms wrapped around the pop tart sensation that has taken all of Whitney Briggs by a shit storm—LeAnn Cleo.

"Oh my, God," I whisper totally caught off guard by the coital brand of affection taking place on the makeshift stage. "*That's* her?" It can't be. What would LeAnn Cleo want with a loser like Aiden? Then again, *I* wanted him—badly at one point. But I was a beaten dog, and, by and large, beaten dogs will stray to anyone who gives them the proper amount of affection.

"Yes! That's *LeAnn Cleo!*" Baya explodes like a piñata bursting into tiny bits of happiness that I'm sure Bryson will chase around trying to lick up with his tongue.

"Oh, no," Laney moans, collapsing her arms around my shoulders once she spots the cheater fawning over the has-been country crooner.

"Crap." It comes from me as more of a statement than an expletive, although I'm sure in about five minutes, I'll rectify that.

"No, really. It is her." Baya goes on. "Look at all that long, blonde hair and those giant blue eyes, she's like an Anime character come to life, right? She's a real scene stealer, so I can totally see how the two of you are blown away right now."

"She's a boyfriend stealer." It grits through my teeth. "And I'm guessing the only person being blown away is Aiden's dick from her collagen-injected lips."

"That's Aiden?" Baya tones it down a few notches now that she sees the shit parade for what it really is.

"Yes." Laney sighs exasperated. "And, for the record, Rox, he's as much to blame as she is, if not more."

"Give me a minute to wallow in my hatred for the skank. I need to refine it into a perfect brew of revenge before I move onto to the asshole in question."

"Look, maybe we should go." Laney tries to pull me to the door, but I prove immovable.

"Maybe we should stay." I snatch my arm back. "If you want, I can make this a night to remember." More like a night to dismember, but I keep the felony in the making to myself for now.

"What's up ladies?" Bryson comes over and wraps his arms around Baya before peppering the side of her face with kisses. My stomach turns at the sight, mostly because I want that—well, not from Bryson, but from someone who would worship me the way he worships Baya. At the root of all my emotional issues is the major freeze out of affection I grew up with, and that only made me crave it that much more. Ironically, it seems to be the one thing I can never truly have.

Ryder swoops into our tiny circle and replicates the molestation with Laney, and, suddenly, I want to vomit on everybody's shoes because it sucks to be me.

"You don't need a man to define you, Roxy." Laney drills into me with that I-know-exactly-what-you're-thinking look. And she always does.

"Damn straight." I glare at Aiden when I say it, and, to my horror, we make eye contact. He shrinks a little like he's afraid for his balls—and wisely so.

The band starts up, and LeAnn bellows into the microphone, slow and painful as if someone is sawing off her toes with a butter knife, and, suddenly, I see a whole felonious to-do list manifesting in my mind.

"God, he's coming this way!" Laney presses into me as if she were physically ready to remove me from the premises.

Baya waves her hands in the air in front of me as if trying to snap me out of a trance. "Show him you don't need him by getting the hell out of here. There's nothing he has to say that you need to hear."

That's for sure, but a little part of me wouldn't mind some groveling from him, perhaps he can offer to sever his dick as a means of restitution? Not that it would be enough. He didn't have much there to begin with.

A quasi-familiar face pops up beside Bryson and flashes a million-watt smile at us.

"What's going on?" The tall, dark, and handsome, buffed out, green-eyed sex God rumbles the words out. "Hey." He holds out a hand, and his dimples dig in deep as he grins at me. "It's about time I get to see my new roommate." The red neon from the Black Bear sign catches his skin and lights up the left side of his face like a warning. His full lips demand my attention, and, for a moment, the rest of the room disappears, taking all the noise and dizzying hormones along with it—it's only Cole and me standing in a vacuum. It feels safe this way, comfortable.

"Not now, Cole." Baya is quick to rebuke his efforts at trying to reacquaint himself with me. We met once, briefly, in this exact same spot about a month ago and haven't laid eyes on one another since.

Aiden weaves through the crowd, cutting both Cole and Bryson a dirty look. He never could stand the thought of me talking to other guys, never mind the fact he took it upon himself to screw other girls. Our relationship was no two-way street.

Cole extends his hand further, waiting for some friendly shake or half-hearted high five to take place. "You mind if I buy you a drink? Maybe we can head out and get some coffee—get to know each other a little bit."

Aiden shoots me a death stare that says you'd better not entertain another penis in my place. His dark features squint with dissatisfaction. Those pale blue eyes of his narrow into judgmental lanterns of hatred.

"Shut up and kiss me." I pull Cole in by the back of the neck, slamming my lips to his, and I go for it. I swallow him whole, swirl my tongue around his mouth as if I were taking up residence, then something in me loosens, and I surrender as he digs his fingers into my waist, his tongue roaming freely in my mouth, slow and deliberate. A soft moan gets locked in my throat as I wrap my arms around his neck and press my body up against the wall of granite that is his chest. It's as if I had found a wormhole in this desperate universe I'm wallowing in, and now I'm transported to some fantastical place I've only heard about, and, ironically enough, the portal was right here through Cole's mouth.

I've only kissed one other boy, and that was Aiden. Clearly this is no boy—Cole Brighton is all man.

An expletive-riddled tirade explodes behind me as Aiden shouts an entire choir of obscenities, I believe I heard the phrase *get the fuck off my girlfriend,* and my chest bucks with a laugh.

Damn it all to hell. Nothing tastes better than revenge—and the flavor of the night just so happens to be Whitney Briggs' own manwhore, Cole Brighton.

Cole

Holy shit.

I dig my fingers into her hips and pull her in tight until I'm crushing her with both my body and mouth. I want to devour her, swallow her down right here in front of every damn person in the bar including the asshole going off like an atom bomb over my shoulder.

As soon as Roxy walked in the place I couldn't take my eyes off her. Who could with that dark hair down to her waist, the I'll-cut-you-if-you-look-at-me-twice attitude. She's the exact opposite of what I'm used to, and I'd be lying if I said she didn't just put my dick on notice.

The uproar continues from behind. A hand plucks me back almost landing me on the floor. I turn to find some idiot in a skintight sweater, his perfect slicked back hair, a signet ring on his finger fixing to imprint itself in my jaw, and I duck.

"Whoa, cowboy." Holt pops up and locks his arms around the douchebag's shoulders. "You're messing with the wrong person. I suggest you leave before we take turns beating the shit out you for fun."

"You can't kick me out. That's my girlfriend up there." He nods to the singer who's screeching away, oblivious to the fact her boyfriend is getting in a scuffle over another girl.

"Which is it?" I knock him in the chest. "Is Roxy your girlfriend or the wannabe rock star who can't hit a high note?"

"Shut the hell up!" He struggles to charge me, but Holt still has him on lockdown.

"That's it, you're gone." Holt twists the little shit toward the exit.

"No, let him stay." Roxy hisses in his face. "I wouldn't want him to miss a moment of his precious *girlfriend* and her craptastic career as a glorified belly dancer. I'm out of here." She charges for the door, and I bolt after her.

"Hey"—I try to block her with my body, but she maneuvers around me—"you don't have to leave."

Roxy keeps walking as if she didn't hear me, and I follow her right out the door into the fresh night air.

"Seriously"—I pull her back by the elbow—"let's get back in there. I swear, I'll deck him if he gets within ten feet of you."

"*You* get back in there." She snatches her arm from me. "I'm done. And don't think I'm signing up to be your fuck buddy just because we kissed. I'm sick of guys like you who treat girls like dirt."

Dirt? I mouth the word, stymied by her point-blank analysis.

"Go find yourself a whore for the night," she screams. "I wouldn't want your sheets to get cold." She takes off for the parking lot, and Baya bolts after her.

"I'm coming with you!" my sister shouts. "You don't have a car, remember?"

I shake my head. Roxy's so blind with rage she can't see straight. I'll be lucky if she doesn't set *fire* to my sheets. Not that I wouldn't mind burning up the mattress with her. Roxy's a little firecracker. I'm sure she's capable of teaching my dick a lesson or two in bed.

I flex a dull smile. Something tells me the last thing Roxy wants to do is teach me or my dick a lesson. Nope, she's all piss and vinegar and both me and my man parts had better steer clear before we get burned.

But she's unsettled something inside me that I haven't felt before, and I can't quite put my finger on it.

I don't treat girls like dirt.

Do I?

৪৩৫৪

The Black Bear is still pumping and jumping by the time I make my way inside. I belly up to the bar just as Holt slides me a cold one.

"You all right?" He gives me that menacing look that suggests he's ready and willing to kick some ass in the event I'm not.

"Yeah, man. It's good. She took off." I nod my beer toward him before knocking it back.

A hard slap lands over my shoulder as Bryson crops up next to me. Bryson and Holt are fraternal twins, same face, or at least as close as you can get without being identical. After a few beers, they tend to morph into one person.

"That was some kiss." He glares at me like I did something wrong.

"She came at me, dude. I did what any red-blooded American boy would do. I kissed her back."

"Yeah, well, her brother wants me to knock your teeth in if it happens again." He glances over his shoulder into the tight knit circle of bodies rocking out to LeAnn. "I'm not kidding. He was ready to follow Rox home and clear her shit out of your place. Keep your paws off, dude. She's a no-fly zone."

I lean my elbows onto the bar. "I don't know. She's got it going on. I can't say I'd fight her if she came at me in the middle of the night."

Bryson knocks his beer into mine. "I'll pretend I didn't hear that."

I twist in my seat and take in the crowd. Nothing but a sea of coeds I've already bagged on a loop.

Crap. I have to admit it was fun at first—girls lining up outside my bedroom to take a spin on my lap, and, God knows, I didn't fight it. Before long, it was two on one, and I didn't mind that one bit either—until it got a little old—not that I've been turning down any opportunities. But somehow, someway, I've become this thing, this insatiable creature that needs sexual gratification before and after classes.

One of the last things my dad said to me was that I shouldn't saddle myself down too young, that I should shop around and when "the one" came along, I would know it, and everything would fall into place. It was the last conversation we had before he went out on that fated bike ride where a drunk driver came and knocked him into kingdom come.

A pair of cold fingers give the back of my neck a squeeze.

"Boo!" An annoyingly high-pitched voice, that could only be one person, giggles into my ear.

It's Angel I-don't-know-her-last-name-don't-want-to.

I tweak my brows at Bryson as a cry for help before turning around.

"What's up?"

She spins into me, lashing me with her whip-straight hair. Her bony arms find a home around my waist. "So, you wanna dance?"

I glance over at Bryson just as he heads into the crowd. Holt is already at the other end of the bar. Great.

"I'm not really the dancing type, sweetie." I gently pluck her hands off my waist and look out in the sea of skirts to find my next victim.

"You sure knew what you were doing under the sheets." She gives my balls a tweak, and I jump in my seat.

"Whoa, watch the boys would you?" I carefully extract her hand from my crotch. Not my usual MO with a girl.

Her eyes squint to nothing as she strings out a giggle. "You really were great. I mean, not that I have anything to compare you with seeing that it was my first time." She saws out a laugh like the braying of a horse.

"Excuse me?" I couldn't have heard her right. I have a strict no-virgins policy. I'm more interested in playing with the pros than I am in training a rookie. "You're kidding, right?"

She takes an uninvited sip from my beer and makes a face. "Skunk juice!" She shoves it back in my chest, and I gingerly place it on the bar. "So what should we do tonight?' She hops into my lap when she says it.

"You still haven't answered my question. About that virgin thing, you're just shitting me, right?"

"No." Her eyes round out like a pair of silver moons. "I mean"—she screeches out a laugh that makes my ears wish they could bleed just to alleviate the pressure—"I *was*." She does her best impression of a bobble head doll. "But you took care of that tiny little detail." Her finger finds a home in my gut, and I kindly remove it. "Anyway, if you don't want to dance, maybe we should leave. We could catch a movie at your place—or think of something a little more exciting to do." Her tongue does a revolution over her lips as she tickles my nose with her finger.

Crap. A virgin? This is definitely new territory for me. I didn't even sleep with a virgin when *I* ran the bases for the very first time.

"Look"—I hop off my seat and hold my hands out like the cherry-popping criminal I apparently am—"I swear I didn't know it was your first time. I would have bought you flowers first." Probably not, as evidenced by the fact I'm eyeing the exit. A movie at my place sounds pretty good right about now—alone.

"*Aw.*" She pulls me in by the collar. "You're a perfect gentleman, aren't you?" Her eyes squint down to nothing. She nibbles on her bottom lip like a bunny, and as much as I'm not into virgins, I'm not into animals, and that's exactly what this not-so-angelic being is shaping up to be.

"Actually, I think I need to get going. I have a roommate that just moved in, and I'd like to get to know her a little better."

"I'd love to see a few more of *your* moves. Why don't we go back to your place, and you can get to know *me* a little better?" She pulls me out the door, and before I know it, she's riding shotgun in my truck.

What the hell, it's just for tonight.

What's it going to hurt?

𝕭𝕮

About midnight I wander out to the kitchen to grab a cold one and run into Roxy. Her hair is messy, cascading down her back like a dark shadow and her mascara is gently smeared. She's got on a tight tank top, and her tits are perfectly outlined like twin melons begging to be set free. I'd like to set them free. Hell, I'd like to take a bite and see just how sweet that fruit really is.

My stomach spears with heat. Damn, she's hot. And that kiss we shared has been ricocheting like a boomerang in my mind for the last few hours. In fact, I couldn't quite function to capacity with what's-her-face, and we spent about twenty minutes locked at the lips before she finally passed out. Not that I mind. It wasn't her kiss that kept my heart pumping. It was Roxy's.

She grunts as she strides past me, and I step over and block the path to her room.

"Anything I should know about you?"

She winces as if I had crossed the line in the proverbial sand. "You want to *know* something about me?"

"Yeah, like, what's your routine?"

"Let's see." She folds her arms across her chest, her face filled with attitude. "As soon as I get home, I like to unhook my bra."

Nice.

Her eyes narrow in on mine. "Except on weekends when I just plain don't wear one."

This just gets better.

She smirks. "Relax, frat boy, I'm not showing off my nipple piercings just yet."

"Nipple piercings?" This is a must see. "And, by the way"—I touch my finger just under her chin, and her eyes widen like she might bite my balls off—"I'm as much a frat boy as you are a sorority girl. Got that, sweet tits?"

She sucks in breath. "Call me that again, and I'll arrange for a nice, slow death."

I pump a dull smile. "Good night, *sweet tits*." I head to my room before all hell breaks loose.

And something tells me it already has.

2

Sugar Coated Truth

Roxy

A spear of defused sunlight lies over my eyes like a blade, annoying the living hell out of me, so I turn and burrow my head in the pillow. My phone buzzes softly from somewhere on my bed, and I slap around until I locate the damn thing. It's Camilla Gorilla Grant, some girl from my old dorm who believes women who shave are simply bending backward to please the opposite gender—that it's our God-given right to be as hairy as nature intended. Nevertheless, she's met the mountain man of her dreams because, apparently, my mother was right when she said every pot has a lid, except for me, of course. I had one of those stupid glass lids that shattered a few weeks back right along with my heart.

"Hello?" I bark at her for interrupting my marathon-sleeping spree.

ADDISON MOORE

"Well hello to you, too." She giggles because apparently college girls are required to laugh after every sentence that utters from their lips. I didn't get the memo. "Hey, like, you're not just getting up right now, are you? It's like eleven-thirty." Also, in order to qualify as a Whitney Briggs coed, you're required to pepper your conversation with the word *like*—like aggressively. And there's that whole Ugg boot requirement, but I've been known to live in mine, so I'll keep that one out of the equation for now.

"No—*yes*, who the hell cares about my nocturnal comas. What do you want?"

"All right, *geez*. I just wanted to put in an order for a little get together I'm having Saturday night."

I sit up, suddenly fully awake with my heart racing at the prospect of filling my very first order. And, God, she asked *me* and not Melanie I-bake-orgasms-by-the-dozen Harrison. It feels like a Christmas miracle about a week too late, but, hell, I'll take it.

"So what are you thinking?" My voice rises a few notches as I try to manufacture something just this side of friendly from my vocal cords.

"Oh, I don't know...It's for Jessa Hopkin's bachelorette party."

"Jessa's getting married?" Great. It was bad enough all my friends were seemingly leashed to their boyfriends— soon they'll be leashing themselves to their boy toys for life.

34

I guess I'd better start that cat rescue I'm destined to run from my home.

"You didn't know? She just got like knocked up and shit, and her parents are all like well you should probably get married, so they're doing it."

"That's a good reason." I don't bother hiding my sarcasm.

"I know, right? It's totally romantic. I mean her baby gets to be a part of her special day. It's a memory she and Brian will always cherish."

"And don't forget the wedding night. That cute little bugger in the making gets in on that fun, too. Hey, wasn't she dating Luke like forever?" Okay so I let one slip, but it's early, and I cried myself to sleep over that entire I left you for LeAnn can't-sing-for-shit Cleo, so I'm allowed to say *like* however the hell much I want today.

"Yeah, but he's not that into her now that she's knocked up with Brian's kid. Guys are funny that way. Once they see you're sleeping with someone else, their dick gets the hint, and you're done. Plus it's like the worst way to kill their ego."

"Ego...right." I chew on that little nugget for a while. If Aiden is anything, he's all ego. He's all about looks, name brands, social standing, and apparently bedding down ageing pop princesses. Come to think of it, he's all about the things that reasonable people abhor.

Camilla puts in her order, and it's only once we get off the phone do I realize that tomorrow is Saturday, so I haul ass out of bed and head for the shower. The door is shut, and the water is running, so I guess I'm out of luck for now. I turn around and smack into a lean side of beef.

"Hey." Cole's eyes widen for a moment. They're the perfect shade of algae—the furry kind you find under a rock, or if I want to get romantic I'd say the color of sweet spring grass right after the rain—*eh,* I think I'll stick to algae. "You sleep okay last night?"

It's funny how he can make even an innocuous question seem like a cheesy pickup line.

A female voice starts in on a bad rendition of *Titanium* from the shower, and I roll my eyes at how clichéd she is without even realizing it.

"Let me guess, she's trying out for the a cappella group on campus? The Saved By the Bellas?" I avert my eyes. She won't make it. I had indigestion that strummed a more bearable rhythm in my stomach last night.

"What?" Cole cinches back like I decked him.

"It's a *Pitch Perfect* reference."

"A Pitch what?" He follows me into the kitchen as if I cared.

"It's a movie, moron—an American classic in the making, sort of like *Mean Girls* which is what *I* am in the event you haven't noticed." I snarl at him. He winces as a low-riding smile plays on his lips, and my insides pinch with heat. His face is peppered with just enough stubble to make kissing him seem interesting—not that it wasn't last night. "Anyway, yeah, I slept like a baby." Right after I cried like one.

Cole steps in between the fridge and me. His blazing eyes bear into mine, and my stomach drops as if I were on a roller coaster. "So what was the deal with you and that guy last night?"

"He took a shit on my heart. The end." I swoop around him and pluck the creamer from the fridge before starting up the coffee maker. Sacks of flour clutter up the counter, and I know I've got enough eggs and butter, so I'll only have to pick up a few odds and ends at the grocery store. Which is a good thing because I'm down to my last few dollars.

Cole steps in front of me with his rock-solid chest inches from mine. "Sounds harsh." His dark hair is slightly rumpled, glossy and black as a raven's wing. He smells like musk and last night's romp and stomp, and yet my insides revolt against my will and have some overt sexual reaction to him. Pathetic. No wonder every girl on campus needs to ride the Brighton express. Nature has turned him into a fundamentally perfect procreation machine, and it's all the opposite gender can do but fall under his primal spell. It's biology, stupid.

"It is harsh, but that's what I get for believing in fairytales." I zip around him and take a seat at the bar while the coffeemaker burps to life.

He leans in across the counter, elbows down, his eyes still trying their best to fuck mine. "What's a fairytale?"

"Love." I don't hesitate with the answer, mostly because it's true. "What you do is real."

Cole flinches as if I had accused him of grand coital larceny.

"You know—you hook-up." I shrug. "You fuck the night away and let the vaginas fall where they may. Nobody expects anything from you."

His head ticks back a notch. His features reconfigure with a look of confusion. Clearly, I've stunned him with this non-revelation.

"What the hell are you talking about? First you tell me I treat women like dirt, then you tell me nobody expects anything from me. I don't treat anyone like dirt and..." he racks his brain for a minute. "My professors all expect things from me—papers to be exact." His lips curve in a victorious smile—a pittance of one at that.

"Oh, come on. Have you not seen the damage you've inflicted on that wall back there with your claw mark collection? I'm surprised you haven't compromised a support beam. I bet the entire building is in danger of collapsing with your next conquest."

He flexes his lips just south of a smile. "All right, so I like to keep track. For the record, since Bryson called off the competition, I haven't added a single scratch to that wall. This isn't some race to see who can land the most chicks."

"No, it's about sex. And, believe me, I appreciate your honesty."

"I take it that idiot last night was anything but."

"That idiot is none of your business." I hop down and pour myself a cup of battery acid the coffeemaker managed to piss out.

"I don't know about that." Cole comes over and rakes his breath over my neck. "It sort of became my business when he tried to split my face open."

I spin around and spill my muddy coffee just shy of his feet. "Boy, you like to get up close and personal, don't you? Let's initiate a new rule, a three-foot clearance around one another at all times." I make my way back to the fridge and hear the pipes twist off in the bathroom.

"Three-foot clearance?" He comes up behind me, and the heat from his body emanates to mine. "It's gonna be pretty hard to recreate that kiss we shared with a buffer like that." His hot breath smooths down my back like a wild fire, and an involuntary moan rips from my throat. "If you want, we can hang out later. I'll let you take that wooden spoon off the wall and chase me around with it. Or maybe I can spank you with it and teach you a lesson?"

I come to and suck in a quick breath. Cole Brighton is nothing short of a carnal magician who's skilled in the fine art of landing coeds on their backs. Well, not this one.

"Look"—I plunk down what's left of my coffee and spin into him—"you can save the one-liners, the bedroom eyes, and the sexual sleight of hand for someone else, buddy." I get right in his face, and my body turns to liquid. "I'm not buying it," I shout, trying to convince both him and my weak feminine needs that I freaking mean it.

He gives a quiet huff, his chest bouncing with the idea of a laugh. "Listen, sweetie, if I wanted you, I'd have had you last night—*all* night." He walks away, and I see nothing but a wall of red.

"*Ha!*" I belt it out, loud and proud. "In your dreams. The only way you can land a girl on the mattress is to get her nice and toasted first. I bet there hasn't been a girl in your bedroom within legal alcohol limits in years."

"Oh, really?" He turns around. "A hundred bucks says you'll be sober the day you beg me to take you back there."

Gah! "You're incredulous!" I strut over and jab my finger in his granite-like chest. "I hate to be the one to break it to you, but you're not all that. In fact, none of the girls at Whitney Briggs think so either." Okay, so I might be making shit up right about now, but, in my defense, my ego demands it.

"Yeah, right." He averts his eyes out the window and somehow this initiates a boiling rage inside me.

"I *am* right." I tilt into that cocky grin brewing on his lips. "You're nothing but a novelty around here just like an ugly sweater at Christmas. No one really wants to be seen with you—you're just a part of the sorority-girl tradition— some hazing ritual that involves the lower half of your body." I glance down a moment before forcing myself to revert back to his eyes.

He shakes his head, completely unaffected by the barb I just threw.

"All right, sweetie. You're still pissed about last night, and I bet you haven't been laid in weeks, so I'll let this one slide." His lips come in close to my cheek, and I inch back just as he comes in for the kill.

His squeeze box left over from last night bops into the room and locks her limbs around him as if she were ready and willing for round two. But I don't stick around for the show. I make a beeline for the shower then get the hell out of dodge.

I've got three-dozen penis cupcakes on order, and I damn well better get used to having a dick in my face especially if I'm going to be living with one.

Cole

It took an hour and a half before I finally convinced Angel to take off. Okay, so I might have treated her like dirt a little, but that was only because she was forcing me to break all sorts of one-night stand bylaws I didn't even know I had. For starters, I'm still a little miffed about the no-virgins infraction. Secondly, no double dipping in a twenty-four hour period or said girl might be led to believe things were "evolving." Third, no working in breakfast, lunch, or dinner around any mattress moves I might be willing to employ. This is just fucking. That's why they're called one-night stands and not relationships. There's a fine line between the two, and I'll be the last to cross it.

I hit the gym over on campus and meet up with Bryson in the weight room.

"Dude." He offers up a fist bump. "Thanks again for standing up for Roxy last night. Sorry things got ugly."

I take a seat on the bench next to him and pluck the towel from around my neck.

"Yeah, well, it seemed like the right thing to do." That conversation we had this morning runs through my mind, more like a screaming match. "What's with her, anyway? She's lit like a match half the time. I tried to be nice to her this morning, and now I'm half afraid she's going to slap me with a sexual harassment lawsuit."

He chuckles, returning his weights to the bar. "Roxy's a head trip sometimes. Tread lightly."

"She mentioned that asshole broke her heart. You know anything about it?"

"He cheated. The end." He unties his shoes while sweat beads down his face. "I guess he and Rox had been together for a while. It wasn't the first time he stepped out on her."

"Really?" I adjust the weights. "I wouldn't have pegged her for someone who put up with too much bullshit."

"I guess you never know what makes someone tick. We've all got our reasons to keep those negative vices around. Speaking of vices"—he stands and stretches his arms over his head—"I've got an opening at the Black Bear if you want it. We've had three bartenders graduate and leave Hollow Brook for greener financial pastures."

"Bartender, huh?" Not that I'm in a position to be choosy. I'm pretty damn strapped at the moment. "I'll take it."

"Great, you can start tomorrow night." He slaps me five on his way out the door.

"See you there."

Bartender. I shake my head. Who am I kidding? The way I log hours at the Black Bear, it's been destined to happen.

"What's up?" A tall guy with a slightly familiar frown takes Bryson's spot, and I nod over at him still unable to place him. "I'm Ryder." He holds out his hand, and I shake it. "Roxy's brother."

That's where I know that frown—runs in the family.

"Oh, right. You were there last night." Suddenly I feel like forfeiting my workout routine. If he's anything like his sister, I'd better put my balls on notice because they're about to get sucker punched.

"Thanks for sticking up for my sister."

"I wasn't really sticking up for her." I throw my leg over the bench and eye the exit. "I was just defending myself from some wasted asshole. What did she ever see in him, anyway?"

"What does anyone see in anyone? Look, Aiden's not her anything, never was never will be. He showed her some attention when she needed it, and the rest is breakup, makeup history that spanned three long years. I'm glad she's finally got him out of her system."

"Dude, why'd you let it go on so long?" My insides clench at the thought of that asswipe screwing with her heart for three years straight.

"Why did I *let* it?" He sits up with a laugh buried in his throat. "I can no sooner stop Roxy from doing anything than I can stop my hair from growing. It's pretty clear you don't know my sister. She can be hardheaded sometimes."

"I got that."

"Yeah, well, what you don't *got* is the fact she's broken on the inside. Look, I'm not getting into it with you, but just know that our family life wasn't as ideal as the Capwell name paints it to be. She's been emotionally starving since birth, and there's a hole in her heart I'm not big enough to fill. She's like the rest of us. She just wants someone to genuinely care."

"Genuinely care." I repeat as if I were taking mental notes on how to navigate the minefield that is Roxy Capwell. And why does Capwell sound so damn familiar? I'll have to implement my ninja google skills once I ditch this place.

"The only reason I'm telling you this is because you're living with her. Do me a favor—don't make any moves on her. She's a little vulnerable right now, and I'd hate to see her thrown into some rebound relationship with the school sex mascot." He flexes a dry smile. "No offense."

Sex mascot?

"No offense taken." I slap him some skin and get the hell out of the gym.

Judgmental prick.

But a part of me knows he's right.

ಐಚಿಚ೫

By the time I get back to the apartment the entire place is lit up with the scent of sugar and spice and, holy shit, everything nice.

Who the hell is this girl? And how did I get so lucky?

"It smells like heaven." I groan as I magnetize toward the kitchen. It's as if a sugar plant exploded and drenched the air with its sickly-sweet affection, and, holy hell, do I ever approve.

Roxy's hair is spun in a knot with a wooden spoon driven through the beautiful mess. Her face is coated with powder. The entire kitchen looks as if a flour bomb went off, but her eyes glow like two backlit beacons warning me not to get too close or me and my dick will run aground faster than we did before.

I step in close behind her and lean in with my cheek less than a breath from hers. The warmth from her skin radiates over mine, and it takes a lot more effort than my testosterone-laden brain can muster not to steal another kiss off those pillow-soft lips.

I swipe my finger through the batter and jam it in my mouth, moaning hard into her ear. Tastes like heaven.

Roxy takes a breath, expanding her back over my chest. I go with it and tuck my lips into her vanilla-scented neck.

She flicks the fork in her hand, and a glob of batter blinds me.

"Crap."

"I never miss." She glances down at my crotch. "Don't you forget it."

"Maybe I don't want you to miss. Maybe I want you to make it hurt." I lick the batter off the side of my hand. "Maybe I'm falling in *love*," I tease.

I lean in close, hoping she'll take the hint and land those luscious pink lips right over mine, but something says she won't. Her eyes widen, her breathing picks up as if she's considering it before her features harden, and my dick shrinks for even entertaining the idea. Damn—this girl is bringing me to my knees, and I'm not sure I like it.

"Love is a two way street, and this street isn't going in your direction." Her chest bucks as she jabs her fork back into the cake mix.

"Hey—what's wrong?"

"My mixer blew out." She flicks a finger at an old wiry looking piece of enamel slumped over itself.

"I think I saw something like that once in my grandmother's kitchen."

"What's that supposed to mean?" She heads toward a shitload of cupcakes laid out across the counter. They're black and blue at the bottom with half of a crooked building spearing out of them.

"It means stop trying to be a hipster and cook with antiques," I say. "Go out and buy one of those overgrown muscle mixers that look as if they could grind out an entire bakery." I scoop up a cupcake and take a bite out of the curved appendage before plucking one of the blue marshmallows off the base and popping it in my mouth. "Mmm, this is fucking good."

A tiny giggle emits from her, and my body relaxes for the first time since we've been together. I think her brother was right, she just needs someone to show her a little kindness, encourage her a bit.

Roxy knocks her head back and breaks out into a full-blown cackle.

"What's so funny?"

"You." She drills those glowing eyes into mine, and my hard-on ticks to life. Roxy is a goddess in the kitchen, and she doesn't even know it. "I think it's hysterical watching the pussy cat king take a big ole bite of dick."

"What?"

"That cupcake. It's a—"

"Shit!" My fingers open voluntarily, and the phallic confection flies to the floor.

"And how did you enjoy those blue balls?" She fingers an innocent marshmallow died sky blue, and I think I'm going to be sick. "All right here's the deal. From now on I'll let you inhale my test batch, and you can tell me if they're poison." Her lips expand in a line. "And for you, they might be."

"Cole?" A whiny high-pitched voice emits from the hall, and I freeze. My eyes widen to the size of silver dollars, and I shake my head at Roxy because I'm pretty sure I'd rather graze over her naughty muffins all day than deal with who I think it is.

"That's right, *honey*." Roxy bites down on her cherry-stained lip. "You have a guest waiting for you in your bedroom." She jabs her finger in her cheek. "I'm sorry, I must have forgotten to tell you."

Angel skips in and oohs at the pornographic plague taking over the counter.

"Mind if I do?" She squeals at the penile confections.

Roxy shakes her beautiful head, and I suddenly wish it were only me and her standing in this kitchen. "Be my guest."

Angel locks eyes with mine before diving her mouth over the phallic extension and taking the head off in one swift bite. "Mmm." She picks me up by the hand, leading me toward my room. "Now let's get to bed."

Crap.

I've got a bona fide level five cling-on to contend with.

Roxy snickers away in the kitchen.

I *bet* she thinks it's funny.

3

Bitter Sweet

Roxy

The women's auxiliary league requests your youthful touch for the Valentine Benefit. Please consider. Let's do lunch.

I sit and stare at the awkward text from my mother. Only she can make an unassuming text sound like a formal invite inscribed with gold foil over parchment. I feel pretty bad about ignoring my own mother, so I text back a quick, **yes,** before my neurons fire on all pistons and realize the malfeasance I've just caused. Granted it was an unenthusiastic yes. The last thing I want to do is embed myself in the auxiliary league. The next thing you know, I'll be wearing pillbox hats and autumn rose lipstick just like Mom is prone to do.

I glimpse at the calendar on my phone. It's New Year's Eve, and both Baya and Laney are dragging me to the Black Bear tonight to witness a bunch of coeds getting drunk off their asses only to ring in the New Year with synchronized vomiting.

I roll out of bed with my eyelids gritting together like sandpaper and stagger my way down the hall, careful not to fall into Cole's den of depravation lest I get entangled in one of his nightly orgies. Well, that's not quite true. After the Angel fiasco last week, he's had a few special "visitors" but they seem to have left as quick as they came. It makes me wonder about his rumored sexual superpowers. I thought, the way the girls were lining up around the block, he had enough in him to make it last all night, but, by the looks of things, he's nothing more than a quick prick.

My eyes spring open for a second. God, I almost forgot that Valentine's is the day after the Sticky Quickie baking competition. I really need to start gearing up and baking myself into a sugar coma if I want to walk away with the ten thousand dollar prize, not to mention the internship at the Sticky Quickie bake shop. It's the steppingstone I need to launch into cupcake superstardom, plus it will give me the edge once I open my own shop. I can practically see the framed sign in the window, *Winner of the Sticky Quickie bakeoff. Voted best cupcakes in town!* That almost puts a smile on my face.

I push the bathroom door open, and a strangled scream gets locked in my throat as Cole stands straddling the toilet. The sound of his thunderous pissing fills the air, and I gag as I jump back into the hall.

"Hey." He shakes himself off before pulling up his boxers. "Morning."

"See this?" I rattle the doorknob. "It's has a lock. *Use it.*"

"Looks like someone woke up on the wrong side of the bed." A half smile inches up his cheek. His hair is slightly rumpled. He's still wearing those sleepy eyes, and his dimples dig in as if they, alone, were enough of an aphrodisiac to seduce me. They are, but that's beside the point.

"Every side would be the wrong side of the bed if you were on it."

"Very funny." The smile glides right back off his face. "I've got about a dozen girls who would contest that fact right this minute."

"And I bet they're all in your room ready and waiting for you to get back from your little trip to the potty. Now, if you don't mind, get the hell out. I need to shower. I've got a million things to do, and not one of them includes holding a conversation with a walking dildo."

His head ticks back an inch. You'd think after a week of dispensing my best comebacks at him, he'd be a little tougher to impress.

"I don't think there are any clean towels." He laments while opening the cabinet under the sink. "I'll try to get to the laundromat later. You can use my towel if you want. I subscribe to the ass-tag system, if you don't mind returning the courtesy."

"The what?" Now I'm the one stymied. Apparently stupidity is running rampant this morning around these perverted parts.

"You know"—he plucks at the tag hanging from his threadbare towel that comes complete with gangrene—"you wipe your..." His eyes travel down my body slow as frozen molasses and stop south of my thighs.

"Ass-tag—got it." I hitch my thumb for him and his Neanderthal-like hygiene practices to get the hell out.

Cole steps in close as he edges his way out of the tiny space. His skin radiates like a heat wave in July as he passes over my body, and every inch of me comes to life in ways I've never felt before. I watch as he struts down the hall in his boxer-briefs, tight in all the right places, and wonder what the hell makes Cole Brighton so damn irresistible?

ഇൻഗ

That night, by the time I get to the Black Bear, both Baya and Laney are seated at a small table in the back. I hitched a ride with Cole who's actually working the bar this evening as a "cocktail architect" as he so moronically put it. Holt and Bryson spent the last week training him to become an official mixologist and it's his first night flying solo.

"Break a leg," I say just before we part ways.

Cole steps in close. His bedroom eyes smolder into mine. I had to take a breath earlier when I saw him with his ass-hugging jeans, and inky shirt, per Black Bear dress code. I wanted to tell him he looked good. That I'm sure he would a do a great job tonight, but the bitch that lives inside me is quick to smother the flame of any kindhearted sentiments that may have wanted to spew from my lips.

"I think maybe *break a glass* is a little more appropriate," he whispers right over my lips. "Or at least more my luck." He gives a crooked smile. Something about his self-abasing comment endears me to him, and I'm quick to stomp that little bit of charity out, too.

"Here's hoping for lots of stitches and a staph infection to round out the night." I push my way past him and take a seat at the table with Laney and Baya.

"About time." Baya shoots her brother a look across the bar as if he were truly to blame. "We're just about to start our shifts."

"So how's it going?" Laney almost mouths the words.

I glance over at Cole who has already amassed a mammary-laden harem down at his end of the bar. Poor Holt. Looks like the tips will be down for him this evening.

Cole's a magnet for anything in kitten heels. I swear that man is like catnip.

"I guess it's going okay. I mean, I bake, and he primarily sleeps all day." I leave out the part about me letting him eat half of my test batches this week. I have a couple more catering events coming up, and after that fiasco at Jessa's bachelorette party which will forever be known for its attacking penis cupcakes, I've been trying to figure out new ways of securing fondant sculptures to my cupcakes.

Laney glances over her shoulder. "No, not that." She looks to Baya for a brief second. "You mean you don't know?"

"Know what?" I inch forward.

Baya clicks her tongue. "Of course, she doesn't know. She lives under a rock. Didn't you hear her? She's been baking my brother cupcakes all week."

"Oh please, I'm not above hitting you." I turn back to Laney. "Dish."

"Okay. Brace yourself." She takes a deep breath as if she were doing just that. "Aiden and LeAnn have been voted campus couple of the year."

"It's all over the school paper." Baya nods into this lunacy. "And the WB website has an entire page dedicated to them. I heard a girl in the counselor's office say it was an ingenious marketing strategy for the school. They think

LeAnn, alone, has the power to double applicants for fall, not to mention boost morale with the alumni."

Laney closes her eyes a moment. "God knows we need it after that disaster of a football season."

"Tell me about it." Baya groans as if she actually cared about which direction the pigskin flew.

"Whoa, back up the train. How can they be couple of the year? I'm the one that was stupid enough to linger around Aiden for the last eleven months. How is he getting all the accolades, and all I'm left with are penis cupcakes?"

Laney and Baya root their jaws to the floor for a minute.

Bryson pops up. "Let's do it, ladies. It's time to get this party started."

"It's New Year's Eve, this party isn't getting started until at least eleven-thirty." Baya gives him a quick wink.

"Yeah"—Laney stands—"we were just about to get all existential and exchange resolutions."

Both she and Baya offer half-hugs of condolence before they move along to their respective stations. Bodies fill in the dance floor, and the DJ starts pumping out enough bubble gum rock to rot our brains long before midnight.

"Everything okay?" Bryson lands a hand over my shoulder, and, instinctually, I want to fold into him. Baya is lucky to have someone as kind as Bryson to get her through this shit storm they call life. She chose wisely, unlike me who bared myself to the first bag of balls that seemed even remotely interested.

Aiden and his newly minted girlfriend stride into the bar with her wrapped in fur from head to toe and him in a dark, expensive looking suit. I guess he finally found his sugar momma. Ryder always tried to warn me that Aiden was after Capwell dollars, and now I'm seeing the fiscal light.

"Everything's great," I shout up over the music.

"If you ever need some spare cash, I can always use some help on the weekends."

My gaze drifts over to Cole at the bar, and something warms in me at the thought. It's probably just gas.

"I'm good, but thanks." I try to muster as much enthusiasm as I can, considering he just offered to pay me cash for something I do around the apartment now on a regular basis—bus dishes for Cole.

I spot my sexed-up roommate at the far end of the bar and Cole nods over at me, flashing his million-dollar smile.

A surge of adrenaline spikes through me at the sight of those dimples, and I don't like it at all.

Swear to God if I fall for Cole Brighton, I'll stab my own eyes out with a fork.

He winks over at me, and my stomach bottoms out.

Something tells me it's time to hide the kitchen utensils.

Cole

Bodies ricochet off one another long into the night. The room is dim. The music is ready to blow out both my eardrums, and to make matters worse, I'm sober. Not only am I sober, but I've somehow slotted myself as the dispenser of all that is good and right with the world—beer and vodka.

"Hey, man." Holt slaps me in the stomach with a dishtowel. "How's it going?"

"Going good, dude." I rest my elbows onto the counter. "I never knew you worked so damn hard. Hats off. This is exhausting as shit."

"It's not always like this. I'm pretty sure it's cruel and unusual punishment to start working on New Year's Eve." He nods over to a bevy of beauties at the end of the bar, and they lift their drinks in our direction. "The ladies sure like what they see. Any you care to sample, or, in your case, two or three?"

"Not funny." I glance over to the far corner and spot Roxy standing there with her arms crossed, her death ray of a stare poised out at the crowd like she's ready to impart a mass slaughter. "Maybe I do see someone I like."

He follows my gaze. "Capwell?" Holt shakes out a laugh. "Dude, she's one to stay away from. First of all, her brother won't think twice before ripping your balls off and feeding them to you for breakfast. Second, her parents are both a piece of work in their own right. And, Rox, well she's a walking ball of rage. I'd be afraid to point my hard-on in her direction."

"What about that asshole she dated? It seemed like they were pretty serious."

"That guy?" He nods not too far from Roxy at Aiden and his new girlfriend, the one-woman karaoke show. "He was just after her for her dough, and when he found out her daddy wasn't gifting his dear old daughter a dime, he moved onto where the grass and dollar bills were greener."

"Nice." So basically she's been in the shitter for most of her life, and my heart breaks for her just thinking about it.

I watch as the douchebag she once dated heads in her direction while LeAnn trots off toward the restroom.

"You mind if I take a quick break?"

"Nope. Go right ahead."

I speed over, and a blonde falls into my chest. Her shrill laugh lets me know who it is before she ever looks up.

Angel.

"There you are!" She stumbles to her feet. "I've been to every frat party tonight looking for you!" Her eyes narrow as if she's genuinely pissed.

I may have led her to believe I was headed to a frat party after about the fifth phone call in which she threatened to sit outside my door and stake out the apartment until I got home.

"About that..." I try to maneuver around her, but she sidesteps right along with me.

A string of giggles stream from her chest. "It's like we're dancing!" Her boobs jiggle in rhythm as she hops up and down. "You know, there's something I need to tell you, and I don't think I can wait until midnight." She bites down nervously over her lip.

I scan the corner from over her shoulder only to find that nutcase barking in Roxy's face, and she looks as if she's about to tear down the whole damn building in retaliation.

"Look"—I brace Angel by the shoulders—"there's something I have to tell you, too."

"Oh, goody!" She hops, spiking her stiletto into my sneaker.

Shit.

"I *know*." She gives my ribs a hard squeeze. "Let's both say it at the same time! One, two, three—"

"I'm in love with you!" she shouts over the music, loud enough to echo up to the moon.

"I'm in love with someone else!" I say in tandem, and her face drops. Her eyes round out before filling with tears, and she's doing the nostril thing.

Crap.

"Hey, kid, it's okay." I give her arms a quick rub. "It'll happen for you someday soon, I swear it. A girl like you won't stay single long." Stalkers rarely do.

Her face brightens. "You're right. My mother always said if there was something I wanted badly enough, it would eventually come to me. And my daddy said—"

"That's great." I give her a quick pat as I push my way through the crowd and land in front of the sack of shit that has the nerve to breathe the same air as Roxy.

"And who the hell are you?" He roars it out as if I were simply the latest development in their argument. "Get lost. We're having a discussion."

Roxy steps up. "I'm not discussing anything with you. And, by the way, this is—"

"Her new boyfriend"—I flatten my hand over the idiot's chest—"and if you don't mind, it's almost midnight—we need to practice for the big kiss."

Roxy pulls me in by the waist. "And then we're going to fuck."

My stomach pinches when she says it because God almighty knows I'd like to do just that. Aiden's face bleaches out, and, for a minute, I see both panic and rage brewing in his eyes. Does this douche actually think she's going to sit around pining for him while he moves on? This guy is nothing but an ego on a stick.

"That's right, we fuck a lot." I poke a finger into his chest causing him to stumble back. His eyes slit to nothing.

He pumps a series of quick breaths through his teeth like a bull at the gate. Who knew pissing off her ex could be such serious fun?

Angel starts marching this way, angry and volatile, and most likely loaded with more mommy-daddy stories than I care to stomach.

I pull Roxy in by the neck. "Kiss me."

She bears into me with those ocean deep eyes, and my insides turn to water.

It's like I'm falling.

She lunges at me with those full, ruby lips, and I collapse over her with a kiss that has the power to evaporate every damn person out of the room, and it does with the exception of Roxy.

Her tongue slips into my mouth, and I'm right there to greet it. We take it slow then detonate over one another in a powerhouse of passion. Her soft tits crush up against my chest as I sweep through her mouth over and over.

Holy hell, how could anyone throw away a girl like Roxy?

Aiden the Asshole just made the biggest mistake of his life.

And I have a feeling this kiss is the beginning of the best move in mine.

Holt sends me home at about two in the morning, and I offer Roxy a ride.

"Don't think this is going anywhere." She drones it out like she isn't above drop kicking my balls into the next decade if I try something.

"Likewise, smartass." I give a little smile as I let her into the apartment. Of course, I don't mean it, and I'm sort of hoping she doesn't mean it, either. "Thanks for helping me out. That chick has been closer than my shadow all week."

"Sounds like a problem." She tosses her purse on the couch.

Roxy comes toward me with that I'll-cut-you look on her face but I don't move, hell, I don't breathe.

"If you ever think of landing those lips on me again, I will make sure it's the last kiss you ever share with anyone." Her chest heaves. Her cheeks darken a deep shade of red, calling her bluff.

"Oh, yeah?" I take a step in and push my face toward hers. "If you ever land those lips on *me* again, I'll make sure it's the last kiss *you* ever share with anyone"—a cocky smile cinches up one side, and I can tell it's pissing the hell out of her—"other than me."

Her throat jumps as she swallows hard.

"In your dreams, manwhore." She flops down onto the couch.

I flip on the tube and land on the opposite sofa. It's kind of nice to just hang out with a girl for once, even if she is rabid half the time.

"So what do you feel like watching?" I ask. Roxy is like a faucet. I never know which I'll get, hot or cold. "Rom com? Horror flick? I bet you'd like to see a few zombies lose some body parts."

"Yup, you got me all figured out. After all, nobody knows women like Cole Brighton." She says that last part overly cheery like some goofy ad campaign.

"I didn't mean it like that." I simply meant she looks like the type of girl who enjoys taking a bite out of a person—a big, bloody, painful bite.

"Save it. Watch whatever the hell you want. I really don't care." She twists her hair into a bun then shakes it back out again, and I sit mesmerized by the fluid way her arms move, the way her midnight-colored hair cascades down her shoulders in perfect waves. The apartment still holds the slight scent of vanilla, and I'm strongly associating that smell with Rox and her creamy-looking skin.

"So, what's your major?"

She gives a hard sigh. "Again, no need for one-liners—really I'm cool with just watching TV."

"It's not a one-liner, I want to know. Mine is business. Now it's your turn, that's how polite conversation works."

She smirks at me. Her eyebrow peaks on one side, giving her that sexy-as-hell look that makes my balls ache just a little.

"*Business*—not that it's any of yours." She folds her arms across her chest.

"You don't need to get all defensive over nothing. This is a safe zone. You can let down your hair, both figuratively and literally, around here." Her panties, too, but I leave that part out. "I'm not out to get you." Yet.

Roxy spears me with a look that says I'll twist your dick off if you go there again. "I don't know what the hell you're talking about. This *is* the real me, the wall is up, and it's staying up because I like it that way, so you can stop trying to scale it, and while you're at it, put away your armchair psychiatry. There's no use in figuring me out. I've already tried."

A brisk knock erupts at the door, and neither of us moves.

Shit. If I see Angel on the other side, I might have to ask Bryson to play bouncer, and I haven't done that in months. Then I remember he's not home, and I'm screwed as shit.

The knocking grows increasingly aggressive, so I hop up and glance out the peephole.

Crap. It's Tia and Mia from Victory University—two blondes that aren't even related, and yet they're pretty hard to tell apart. They come around every now and again looking to triple their pleasure, and I'm usually quick to comply. Maybe I'll tell them I've had a rough night, that I just want some damn sleep for once. Not that it's true. I just don't feel like the hookup. Wait, did I just say that?

I crack the door open, and they trample their way inside, giggling and falling like they, too, have bellied up to the bar a good six hours tonight.

"Happy New Year!" One of them screams before blowing into her party horn. They stop short when they see Roxy on the couch. "You didn't start the party without us, did you?"

Roxy drags her eyes from one to the other, and I can practically hear the sarcasm streaming from her lips.

"Trust me, girls, he's saving the best moves for last." She snatches the remote off the table. "Go ahead, cowboy." She shoots me a look. "Corral these fillies into your stall, and take 'em for a ride before one of them pukes on me."

"About that." I pull the girls in and start walking them toward the door. "I was just about to hit the sheets."

"No time like the present!" They sing in unison and bounce up and down like a couple of pornographic cheerleaders.

"I was sort of thinking—"

One of them cuts me off. "She could totally join us if you want." Mia holds a charitable hand to Roxy.

"Yeah, for sure!" Tia sings. "The more the merrier!"

Roxy slits her eyes to nothing. "I'll pass."

"Oh, come on," Mia whines. "Cole knows how to make you feel like you're the only girl in the room." She closes her eyes and moans as if we're already there. "And the things that boy can do with his tongue." She lets out a heated cry, and Roxy rolls her eyes.

Tia smacks her friend in the gut. "She's obviously slept with Cole. Of course, she knows what he can do with his tongue."

"I haven't slept with Cole," Roxy growls it out with venom as if they just accused her of a bank heist. "Nor do I intend to."

"*Oh!*" Mia dips her knees. "You must be a *lesbian*." She claps as if it were a novelty. "Cole can totally change your mind about that whole girl-on-girl thing. He's really got a gift for—"

"Look, I'm not a dyke," Roxy barks it out before reverting her attention to the television. "Believe it or not, there are girls who don't feel the need to bed Cole Brighton, and I happen to be one of them."

The girls straighten in tandem.

"The *only* one," Mia huffs. They smirk at my new roommate before stalking off to my bedroom, incredulous that an anti-Cole supporter has penetrated the inner sanctum. Come to think of it, I'm a little disbelieving myself.

"You'd better get going." Roxy kicks me in the shin on the way to the kitchen. "You don't want to keep your guests waiting. Do what you do best—bang like a screen door in a hurricane." She pulls out a mixing bowl and a bag of sugar.

My chest pumps with a laugh. I guess I could give a hurricane a run for its screen-banging money. The smile melts from my face as I follow her over.

"You eat dinner?" I'm not sure why I asked other than my heart breaks for her just a little the way she's assaulting those ingredients.

"*This* is dinner."

"You know you can't eat that crap every day."

"Oh, yeah?" She looks up with wild eyes. "What do you eat?" She pushes forward an empty fast food bag. "This?" She reaches back and thrusts a pizza box in my face. "*This*?"

"That happens to be very nutritious, it's got bread, a vegetable, and a dairy. That's knocking out three levels of the food pyramid right there."

"Oh, please. Everyone knows the food pyramid is a sham." She looks up exasperated. "Get out of my face, Cole. Go pleasure your harem. I really don't give a shit."

And there's that.

My stomach sinks like a stone.

Wait a minute. Do I care if she gives a shit? My insides churn because, holy hell, I think I do.

"Do you think we could have something?" There I laid it all out. If she says yes, I'll simply kick the girls out. And if she says no, I'll still want to kick the girls out, albeit for a far less justifiable reason.

Roxy turns around, drills those nightlights she calls eyes into mine, and her features soften. "No, Cole, I don't." She reverts her attention back to the mixing bowl, and the air in the room stiffens to something just this side of claustrophobic.

"Yeah, well, I don't either." I have no clue why I threw it out there—maybe saving face. I can count on one hand how many times I've been turned down for anything and still have four fingers and a thumb left over. It doesn't feel good. In fact, it downright feels like shit.

I head over to my bedroom.

I think Rox and I can have something if we give it a shot. That kiss we shared tonight can testify to that.

My bed is already rocking by the time I get inside with two very naked, very wasted blonde bombshells. They scream in a fit of giggles as I enter their midst and land square between them. They start in on the alternate kisses, the ripping of my clothes, but I'm not feeling it. I lie back on the bed, and one of them offers up a quick hand job to get me going, but my dick is busy playing dead.

After about ten minutes, they sit up with a look of sexual frustration in their eyes that I've never seen before.

"Maybe we should go?" Tia fumbles for her bra, and my ego kicks in full throttle. If Roxy sees them leave, it'll take her two seconds to figure out I couldn't get it up.

"I think we should play a game." I reach under my bed, where I know for a fact I have a testament to both Milton Bradley and the Parker Brothers, until I fish out Monopoly. "I call bank."

We play until sunrise, and I make sure the girls giggle up a storm while I stomp the wall with my fist each time I pass go.

No use in letting Roxy think this is all about her. I've never let a girl get to me before, and I'm not starting now.

But too bad for me because I'm already gone.

Roxy Capwell already has me in the very worst way, and, tragically, she's the only girl at Whitney Briggs who doesn't want anything to do with me.

Ego blown.

4

Sticky Situation

Roxy

Marilyn Manson called and ordered two-dozen big top cupcakes. Not *the* Marilyn Manson, the other Marilyn Manson that belongs to my mother's ritzy rotary club. My mother is in more clubs than Cole Brighton is girls.

I let out an audible chuckle. Actually, Cole hasn't had a single girl over for a solid week since the Bobbsey twins rang in the New Year with him. Technically, it was the kiss *we* shared that rang in the New Year. They were simply a supplement to make his dick feel like a hero.

Anyway, if Marilyn likes these cupcakes and word gets out, I'm likely to boom into a full-fledged upper echelon cupcake catering facility. All the who-gives-a-shit-who's-who will want in on my mad sugar wielding skills, and, before I know it, I'll be delivering cupcakes in a fully loaded

Bentley. Well, not really. I'd die before I yakked up that kind of money for a car. In fact, the Hollow Brook rapid transit is perfectly fine at getting me around to wherever I need to be. Besides, I've practically shirked all mass consumerism. I'm Gen-X that way, not to mention a little on the hippie side—peace, love, and all the bullshit that comes along with it.

My lips twist as I examine the pink confections neatly lined in rows of four on the counter, each with a pink gumdrop pressed into the center like a glowing pink nipple.

"Lame," I whisper. I ran out of butter, so I thought I'd see what they looked like if I went without frosting. Melanie Harrison swears up and down that frostless cupcakes are going to be the new rage. That it was all they talked about in pastry school last summer in France, but I'm betting a bunch of four-year-olds aren't going to buy my art nouveau bullshit if I show up to a princess party without a three inch clearance of butter and sugar on top of these bad boys, so I grab my purse and head for the store.

"Hey, girl!" Baya catches up with me as I'm about to cross the street. There's nothing but a clear, blue sky up above, but it's freezing as shit.

"What's up?" She barrels at me with a monster hug. Baya is friendly like that, and I don't really mind. For whatever reason, God smiled, and I don't have an ounce of hatred in my heart for her. I think Laney is the real reason I don't mind Baya. Any friend of Laney's is a friend of mine.

"I was just headed to Hallowed Grounds. Laney's there, wanna join us?"

"Sure. I still have a couple hours before the cupcakes need to be delivered, and I'm all for a decent cup of coffee. Try as I might, I still haven't mastered that one."

"Cole makes a pretty mean cup." She bumps her shoulder into mine.

"I wouldn't know. I'm not one of his hussies, Baya." I try to say it as sweetly as possible, but she's got to know her brother's a douche, right? I mean she *is* the one who pointed out the writing on the wall.

"I never said you were one of his hussies." She pulls me by the hand until we're inside the warmth of the coffee house where the air is thick with the scent of heavenly-roasted beans. If Cole could make the apartment smell like this, I might reconsider my stance on sleeping with him. Wait, what am I saying? Cole Brighton is a walking STD. Hell, he's inventing *new* STD's by the minute. I should be investing in Purell and walking around the place with Lysol in hopes to keep my immune system intact.

"What's going on?" Laney looks genuinely worried for me.

"She denies having feelings for Cole." Baya's teasing, but a part of her is wishing it weren't true. I know all about wanting your BFF and brother to hook up, that's exactly what happened with Laney and Ryder.

"I'm not denying any feelings. I simply don't have them." Something pinches in my chest like maybe I do. "Anyway, I think all this sugar is going to my head. I just stepped out to pick up a few more ingredients for a delivery this afternoon."

"Oh, that's right." Laney perks up. "How's business?"

"Great. I'm averaging three orders per week. And usually one of them involves a penis."

"Nice," Laney sings. "Good weeks usually do."

"That's disgusting considering you're with my big bro."

We get our coffee and take a seat out front under the heat lamps.

"Hey, what's going on over there?" I nod toward the center of campus just shy of the fortress of evergreens that border the property. A camera crew has set up, flocked with dozens of students as a couple stands to the side.

"Crap," Laney whispers. "Is that today?"

"Is what today?" My voice sharpens as I spot an all-too-familiar brown leather jacket standing next to an all-too-familiar pop-tart singing sensation with an overgrown coif.

"Look, we should probably just sit inside. It's pretty cold out here." Laney does her best to herd us back in, but I prove immovable.

"It's them." Aiden and LeAnn hold one another while the camera snaps away. The crowd of students move in a slow blob behind them.

"It's stupid." Laney snatches at my elbow and tries to pull me toward the door, but I hold strong.

"Damn straight, it's stupid, but that looks like it's beside the point. What the hell is happening? Spill it, Sawyer."

Laney lets out a reluctant sigh. "The drama department was asked to show up this morning for a photo shoot." She glances nervously at Baya. "They're redoing all of the university promo shots using Aiden and what's her face."

Baya heaves as if she's just been sucker punched, but really it's me who's had the wind knocked out of her.

"So—*what*? They're representing the entire damn school?" Just the thought of seeing their smiling faces stamped all over campus makes me rethink my enrollment.

"Something like that." Laney's shoulders drop. "I'm really sorry, hon. I wouldn't blame you if you wanted to throw things or cry."

"I don't cry." I spit it out so fast I almost believe it. I don't cry in front of *people* that is. I'm not opposed to letting the waterworks loose in my bedroom. "So what's new with you guys?" I try to fake interest, but the fact is I want to run over to that photo shoot and dump my scalding hot coffee all over Aiden and his cock's new favorite addiction. I hate that he said he loved me and then turned around and "loved" someone else. I hate that I fell so hard for a boy who I thought could really care about me, and he turned out to be nothing but a player. At least Cole owns his manwhore ways and flaunts them loud and proud for all to see by way of tally marks in the living room. Aiden is nothing but a coward who hid them behind his girlfriend's back.

"Well, now that you've asked"—Baya blushes a severe shade of red—"I did see something on Bryson's laptop the other day when he left the room for a minute."

"God"—I force myself to take an even breath—"if this has something to do with kinky porn, I'm pretty sure I don't want to know."

"No." Baya looks skyward a moment. "God, no. It has to do with engagement rings. He happened to leave the room, and I wanted to look something up—that's when I saw it. He was on *Trevor's* website."

"Trevor's!" Laney's eyes bug out. "That's the engagement ring superstore."

"I know." Baya slaps her hand down on the table.

"Congratulations?" I'm not really sure how to respond to the fact she stumbled on an engagement ring website.

"Thanks." She wiggles in her seat. "Anyway"—Baya glances down, the color rising to her cheeks again—"if he were to ask, of course, I'd say yes."

"I sure did." Laney holds out the golf ball my brother put on her finger and blinds us momentarily.

"So, Laney, what's new with you?" I cross my arms and slouch in my seat because I'm one hundred percent positive I'm about to be treated to more pre-wedded bliss.

"My talent agent called and said there was an open audition for *Invicta* coming up. Ryder, and I have already booked a flight."

"Oh, my gosh, I love that show! Congratulations!" Baya gushes.

"That's great." I lean over and offer a quick hug. I'm not a hugger by nature, but this practically warrants one, plus there wasn't one bit of relationship news attached, so a shallow part of me is forever grateful. "You totally deserve the role," I say. "So when's the big audition?"

"February thirteenth." She presses into her seat and winces.

"What?" I can hardly catch my breath. "But that's..."

"I know." She hides behind her hands for a moment. "It's the day of your big competition. But Baya will still be there."

"I'll need *two* assistants. And they won't be providing any." I sink further in my seat. "And, God knows, I have no other friends. This is going to suck big hairy marshmallow balls."

"I'm sure Bryson would be willing to help." Baya bites down on her lip as if she's sure that's the last thing he'd want to do. "Or how about Cole?" Her face brightens as if he were the solution to all my problems, and, knowing Baya, she believes he is.

"Cole," I grunt his name out, stale as three-day-old bread.

I let out a hard breath.

There goes any hope of ever getting into the Sticky Quickie bakeshop. The only Sticky Quickie Cole Brighton is interested in helping me with happens to be in his pants.

₧ℂℓ

I ended up hanging out with Laney and Baya way longer than anticipated, so by the time I run to the store, pick up my supplies, and get back to the apartment, it's almost time to leave for the bus.

"Hey, good looking." A lewd grin buds on Cole's lips from the kitchen. "Thank you."

"Thank you for what?" I rush over to the counter and spill out my supplies while rinsing the whisk.

"You know, the treat you left me."

I pause for a minute as a million wild thoughts sail through my head at once.

Treat I left him?

Crap. Did I use his towel this morning? Did I forget to ascribe to the ass-tag mentality he attaches to his hygiene products? Maybe I flashed him my boobs while I was walking down the hall this morning. I've been known to do an entire stack of stupid when I'm half awake.

"What treat?" I pull out a mixing bowl and open a fresh bag of confectioners sugar.

"You know"—he strums his fingers over the counter—"the little pink tits."

My muscles freeze.

"What did you just say?" I turn to face him. My entire body lights up like a flame at the prospect of what may have happened.

"The little pink tits. I scarfed down about six of them without milk. They were so freaking good, I couldn't help myself."

"Oh, crap. It's like the whole world is out to get me." I run over and find a sparse half dozen cupcakes staring me in the face. An entire string of tiny wadded up wrappers mock me as evidence of his booby apocalypse. "Those tits weren't for you, Brighton."

"What do you mean they weren't for me? I handle the test batch to see if they're poison, remember?" He shakes his head like a little boy, and something in me melts, except too bad for him because the bitch in me just strangled the shit out of that ridiculous part of me.

"Let me repeat, they weren't for you—and the next time I leave a test batch, they *will* be poison. And *little pink tits?* Really?"

"Yeah, really." He ticks his head back a notch. "Don't look at me like that, you're the pervert who's planting erections in an innocent bed of frosting every time I turn around."

"*Ugh!* Shut up! I suddenly want to plant a very sharp knife in that bed of frosting you call a brain."

"Go ahead and do it, that way you'll get to test out the kitchen facilities behind bars. I bet they have a lot of bake offs you could enter in prison."

He has the balls to reach for another cupcake, and I slap his hand.

Gah! I'm so stupid. I should have left a note letting him know this wasn't a test batch.

A quivering sigh escapes me as I look at the meager row of confections lining the counter. I really needed this.

"Marilyn Manson was my ticket to easy street," I whisper. "As much as I appreciate public transportation, a tiny part of me wouldn't mind a set of wheels to call my own."

"Whoa." Cole jumps up and comes over. Before I know it his hand is roving over my back, his woodsy cologne penetrates the vicinity, and it's not until then do I even realize I miss the scent of a man. "I'm really sorry. Here"—he turns the oven on—"let me help you do this. I want to make this up to you. Two hands are better than one, right?"

"I have two hands, you moron." I push him off me. "If it's one thing I can't stand it's a guy faking nice while he's about to cop a feel. Go find somebody to hookup with, or go shoot black tar heroine or whatever the hell it is you do on a Saturday."

Cole locks eyes with mine and holds me hostage with those neon green traffic lights he sees the world through.

"Maybe I want to hang out with you on a Saturday—or a Saturday night." He lets his words hang out there like an offer.

"I can't date you, you're a porn addict."

"I'm not into porn."

"No, you live it. And, in doing so, you've jacked up your Johnson." He looks simultaneously confused and frightened, so I decide to draw him a picture. "When you put a domesticated pig out in the wild he goes feral within weeks. Face it, you've let your sexual appetite into the wild, and now you're feral. One woman isn't enough for you anymore. You have to work harder to stay stimulated because of your living-porn addiction. Wow, just think how depraved you'll be by the time you're thirty? You'll need ten chicks in bed with you before your dick decides getting it up is worth the effort. Face it, my friend—you've screwed up your dopamine receptors."

"So that's a no on the date, I take it." His dimples press in with the slight look of disappointment.

"*No.*" My chest heaves because, for whatever reason, it was tougher to turn down that date than I thought. "Now just get out, would you?"

"Whatever you want, cupcake." He takes a step into me. Those lush, full lips of his beckon me like some otherworldly aphrodisiac.

"Don't call me that," I whisper.

He takes a step toward me with an animalistic glint in his eye.

His lips twitch with a smile. He comes in close, then closer... His eyes round out as he comes in for the kill. There's a boyishness about him that I find unmistakably attractive, and I wish I didn't. I wish I could say I was immune to all of Cole Brighton's wicked ways, but God knows I'm weak and about to fold. Not to mention the fact that one naked selfie of the two of us tangled up in each other's arms would be a great congratulations-on-your-new-relationship gift to send my ex-boyfriend.

"I think I'm going to kiss you," he whispers right over my lips.

"Relax." I press a hand to his chest and push him away. "I'm not going to kiss you back."

"Why the hell not?" His brows arch so far up into his forehead they almost reach his hairline. Cole looks genuinely stumped by this development.

"Because you like the ladies, remember? And you should probably be neutered." I start in on frosting the cupcakes he christened with an indecent nickname because, God knows, I don't have time to properly explain the order of the universe to Cole *and* get my *little pink tits* frosted in time. "Besides, I'm not interested in a hookup. That's not what I'm about."

Cole picks my chin up gently with his finger and makes me drink down his stare. "Maybe that's not what I'm about anymore either." I watch as he snatches his keys and heads for the door. "Look, I really believe there's a nice person living under that layer of sarcasm." He pauses like he wants to say more but has decided to swallow down his words instead. "I'll be at the gym. Call me if you need a ride to wherever it is you're going." He pauses for a moment. "I promise you, the whole world isn't out to get you, Rox. A lot of people would love to help if you just open up and let them in." And, with that, he walks out the door.

Let them in?

I bet he'd like for me to *open up* and let him *in*.

I beat the shit out of the butter in an attempt to soften it, but, much like my heart, it's a lost cause. It needs to melt slowly, sort of the way Cole is melting me slowly.

But it'll be a cold day in hell when I let Cole Brighton bring my hormones to a rolling boil.

And, unfortunately, something tells me the weather forecast in hell is about to get a little frigid.

Cole

I think I'm going to kiss you?

I haven't uttered those idiotic words to a girl since the fifth grade. And if I recall correctly, it backfired on me then, too. What the hell was I thinking, asking permission? Kisses are the one thing in life it's not cool to ask for. You need to go in with command, take her lips by force, not whine on the sidelines like some pussy while begging for more.

I find a bench near the back of the gym and start loading up the weights. I want this to hurt. I want to feel muscles ripping, tendons shredding. I want all of the frustration of not having a single warm body in my bed for more than seven days straight to be translated into physical pain by way of a quasi-sports injury.

An all-too-familiar blonde gives a spastic wave from the entry.

Angel.

Crap. If this day wasn't already lost in a shit storm, it's about to rain again, and I have a feeling I'm going to be forced to like it.

"Hi there!" She bops over and tries to plant a kiss on my lips, but I turn and avoid the hot pink sticky gloss by mere inches. "Guess what?" She beams with an unrequited amount of joy that nothing short of a visit to the Magic Kingdom, escorted by the head mouse himself should warrant.

"You're transferring out of state?" I mutter under my breath.

"No, silly." She swats me over the shoulder. "My dad and his friends are coming down to stay at the local clubhouse for a while. He's been asking all about you, and I'm just dying to introduce you."

"Your dad?" It's obvious I should be far more afraid for my welfare than my testosterone will allow. This chick is clearly batshit. "I don't think I should be meeting your dad—anybody's dad for that matter. We're not at that level."

"But we can be. Besides, I let him know you were a special friend." Her watery blue eyes quiver as if she were about to unleash the floodgates. Something tells me I should build an Ark, crawl in, and shut the door very fucking tight.

"Angel." I close my eyes for a moment hoping this is all just some bad dream. "I'm sorry if I ever gave you the impression we were together. I swear to you, I'm nothing but a low life. I should be neutered." I can't believe I just quoted Roxy in the most offensive way possible. My balls just shrank three inches in disbelief.

Her mouth falls opens. Her eyes get all weird and squirrely like she's about to cry or throw shit. "What are you saying?"

"I'm saying I'm seeing someone. Which is the exact same thing I said to you New Year's Eve. Look, things are getting serious between my new girlfriend and me. We have very strong feelings for each other." Anger and disgust being the most prominent at the moment.

"Oh, this is terrible." She trembles when she says it as if I had just informed her I was suffering from some incurable disease. "My dad is going to flip when he finds out we're not together."

"Why?" I'm almost afraid to ask. Something tells me the psychotic fruit didn't fall far from the tree.

"It's not important." She bites down on her lip so hard I'm afraid she's going to shoot blood at me any moment now. "Hey, I know—" She twists into me with a mischievous, albeit vapid, glint in her eye. "Do you think you'd mind coming to meet him? That way he could see everything's fine between us. You know, sort of a fake relationship." She gives a slight nod.

"No can do." I happen to have met my quota on those.

Holt strolls in with those beefed up guns of his, already flexing, that golden hair of his swept back and glowing. Surely he's enough to make any sorority girl scream with pleasure.

I nod over to him. "See that guy over there?" She follows my gaze to a poor, unassuming Holt Edwards who's about to have his ass plated up as an offering. "As much I'd hate to pass you off on someone else—if you can't be with me, I'd like to see you with my good friend, Holt. That way we can still be in one another's lives even if it is on the fringes."

She sucks in a quick breath. Her hand claps over her mouth like she might be sick.

"Oh, Cole!" She throws her arms around me in a tragic, yet, violent, embrace. "I knew you cared about me deep down inside. There was no way a man could make love to me the way you did and not care about me as a person."

About a dozen people turn in our direction.

Shit. If ever the earth planned on opening up and swallowing me, now would be a good time to do it.

"What's up?" Holt takes a seat across from me, and Angel jumps a little as if she were being called out on some serious BS. I know for a fact she'll never fall for Holt in a million years because I was stupid enough to land her on the mattress first. Psychos are loyal that way.

"I'll talk to you later." She leans in and plants a wet one right on my cheek. "My dad will be in town for a while, so no hurry in meeting him right away." She starts to head out. "Ta ta for now!" She curls her fingers with a brief wave.

"Thanks, dude." I slap him five.

"I knew you were in trouble when I spotted a three-foot clearance between you two. Stay away from clingy girls, would you?"

"I plan on staying away from every one of the fairer sex—except maybe one girl."

"Roxy finally get to you?"

"How'd you know?"

"Are you kidding? I happened to bear witness to those lip locks the two of you shared at the bar. You do that again and I'm going to have to put out the flames with a fire extinguisher."

"If you saw it, and I felt it, then why the hell is Roxy playing so hard to get?"

"Because you're an idiot."

I whip the towel off my neck and smack him.

"You are," he continues. "She's a girl. If you're interested in her for something more than a one-night stand you're going to have to pull back, start off slow—take her to dinner—share a pizza, have a few heart to hearts before you start jamming your tongue down her throat."

"And how about you? You sharing a pizza with anyone? Are you filling your nights by the fire, talking about how much it hurts to have your balls wrenched by a girl for the very first time?"

"Funny you ask." He blinks a smile. "You know what I'm doing? I'm not looking. You know why? Because that's exactly when fate lets you find the one you're going to spend the rest of your life with." He lies back and starts in on the weights.

A dry laugh pumps through me. I wasn't looking for anyone to share a meal with—anyone to pour my heart out to all night long—and yet something inside of me wants just that with Roxy in the worst way possible.

∓∞∓

Days drift by, and it's almost time for classes to start up again. I remember when I was a kid my dad used to say the older you got the faster the years would melt by with a high velocity, that I'd know the feeling when I had kids of my own one day. But I seem to know it now. After Dad died, it all sort of jumbled into one long dizzying blur of girls. I guess sometimes you can self medicate with people, or in Roxy's case, without.

I wipe down the bar with a marked aggression. Too bad my dad won't be there to see time fly with me or my kids. I'd give anything to have him walk through that door, any door for that matter. It was nice seeing Mom over Christmas. I'm glad she's finally getting back out in the dating pool after years of losing herself in a sea of work, but, in truth, it hurt just a little to hear her say it. For some reason my mind has it that she and my dad will always be together. In my heart I hurt for him just a little when she said she was seeing some guy named Tom. I'd like to see her bring *Tom* around. I'd like to show him a thing or two, starting with my knuckles.

"Hey, slacker." Baya pops up on the stool in front of me.

"You're early."

"My shift starts in ten minutes."

I glance over at the wall clock behind the bar and am shocked to see half my shift has drifted by.

"That went fast. I was just thinking how time seems to fly." I pour myself a cup of ice water and down it to keep my emotions in check.

"You're thinking about him again aren't you?" Baya reaches over and touches my hand. She could always tell when life was getting to me. "Yup. It's a little hard around the holidays."

"Especially when Mom is gushing about her new boy toy." Baya sticks a finger down her throat and mock gags. "That was a little more than I ever wanted to hear. But I get it." Baya sags in her seat. "Mom is only human. And, face it, she's out there in Texas all alone. I know for a fact she's wanted someone other than you and me to talk to for years."

"That's what friends are for, not people named Tom with a dual degree in rocket science and brain surgery."

She gives a little laugh. "She did paint him out to be pretty great, but Mom's pretty great, too. I think she deserves someone like that in the least." She takes a deep breath. "I think Dad would think she deserved someone like that, too."

And there it is, the gut wrenching reality that my sister is probably right.

"I know. It's just hard to picture. I guess I'm a one-man-one-woman-for-life kind of guy."

Baya roars out a quick laugh. "You? Mr. *Scoreboard*? The boy who likes to round out the bases on opening night? Please." She rolls her eyes. Baya is sweet and beautiful and smart as hell—and if she thinks I'm far removed from that reality then I've drifted farther than I think in my quest to have a "little fun" in college.

"Shit." I shake my head. "You think there's any hope for an idiot like me?"

She tilts her head into me, her eyes watering with a heartbreak I can't even begin to understand. "Only you know the answer to that, Cole." She slides off the seat and points across the bar at Bryson. "If anyone can help you figure out a way to be a one woman man it's him."

I shake my head at my old roommate.

Bryson Edwards made it out of the sexual woods alive and with just one girl on his arm. Here's hoping he can show me the way.

Here's hoping Roxy is the girl walking beside me once I'm out.

If Bryson Edwards holds the key, then I damn well better find out what it is.

⚮

After my shift, I hunt down Bryson at his apartment, which happens to be right next to mine.

"Come in."

I haven't been here since I helped drag his stuff over a few months back. It feels weird knowing he defiles my sister in this place. My stomach turns, and I feel lightheaded just thinking about it.

"Grab a seat. I'll get you a cold one." He tosses a water bottle at me before I hit the couch. "What's up?"

"Just checking in." The couch is in a different configuration. The kitchen looks the same sans the cooking clutter, but then I'm pretty psyched each time Rox churns out a batch of fresh cupcakes, so I don't mind the clutter so much. "I think I'm into Roxy." There, I said it.

"Really?" He presses back into the sofa, amused.

"Yeah, really. You got a problem with that?"

"No. Ryder might, but I don't. I think Roxy is a great girl. She has her rough side, but if you don't get under her skin you might survive. Ryder's a great guy too once you get to know him, but he's pretty protective, so you might want to lay low at first."

"Like you did." Baya and Bryson kept their relationship a secret from me for who knows how long. "I'm not big on sneaking around. Besides, she hasn't exactly reciprocated. I'm just wondering how I might convince her I'm being genuine. I've got a scoreboard on the wall that says maybe I'm not."

"You still adding to it?"

"No." I stop shy of telling him I've lost my boner for the masses. "I'm sort of stuck on Rox." I take a breath. "I'm pretty sure I'm done with that thing forever. I'm not into notches or other people's crotches. I want something more." A picture of Baya and Bryson encapsulated in a frame catches my attention. "I want what you and my sister have."

"You should tell her."

"She's going to think I'm trying to land her on her back." Not that I'm opposed to that position. It happens to be my favorite. I'm old fashioned that way.

"Tell her you want to take it slow—and *mean* it." He growls it out. "I get you're into her, but you're still you. I think if you want to build something that lasts, you need to start at the beginning, and the bedroom just so happens to be at the tail end. That's what Baya and I did."

"Whoa." I touch my hands to my ears before getting up. "I think I've heard enough." I offer him a knuckle bump. "Thanks, man."

I take off and close the door behind me.

I'm glad Baya is with a great guy like Bryson. I don't think I could have picked anyone better for my sister. And one day I'd love to hear Ryder say the same thing about me.

Slow.

Something tells me it's going to kill me just a little bit.

5

Butter Me Up

Roxy

A week thumps by, and winter starts in on her brutal assault, turning the walkways, the grass, the pine trees into frosted confections handmade by the supreme baker in the sky. It may be pretty to look at, but it's cold as hell with a biting wind that cuts right through all ten layers of clothing I've piled on today.

Whitney Briggs has its fair share of fashion-minded coeds who run around looking like snow bunnies begging to get laid by the big bad abominable snowman—I'm presuming that's Cole—although, he's been off his game as of late. It's as if that sugar coma I inadvertently launched him into has put his dick on notice, letting him know that maybe I do want a bite out of him after all. His thick-barreled biceps run through my mind—his tattoos laid out like a map that I'd like to trace with my tongue. Those long lashes, those sexy-as-hell lime green eyes that electrify me every time he walks into the room are about all I can handle. If I didn't hate anything on this planet that has a procreative organ outside its body, if I didn't hate men who shared their bed with more women than there are grains of sand on a California beach, then I actually think my vagina and his penis might be paired quite nicely.

I give a smug grin at the thought as I make my way to my first class of the day, Entrepreneurship and Small Business. I'm pretty psyched about this class for two reasons; one, I plan on opening up my own store as soon as I get out of this hellhole, and, two, I've sort of already started my own business right from the comfort of my very own apartment. Of course, one day, I hope to acquire an actual storefront. I'll probably have to grovel to Ryder and beg him to cosign a loan for me, but I'm ready and willing to work very hard and pay back every red cent. If it's one thing my parents instilled in me it's to live debt free whenever possible. Another thing they've made clear as Waterford crystal is that once I graduate, I'm permanently cut off from any Capwell funds and free to make my own way in the world. It sucks knowing that all of the wealth my parents have amassed will be hitting the road once they croak to about a dozen different charities. Not that I'm opposed to helping charities, it's just that I'm not so sure I'd leave my kids high and dry. I kind of like the idea of helping them get on their feet, helping them out with say a *bakery* if need be. Not that I want my parents to croak. I love them despite all the bullshit we've been through. I just plan on being a different kind of parent.

I run up the steps to Burgundy Hall where the business classes are held.

That's funny, I don't think I've ever thought about having kids before. An entire army of dark-haired boys with piercing green eyes flutter through my mind, and, alarmingly, they all look like doppelgangers of my sexed-up roommate.

Pft. As if.

I try to shake the thought out of my head, but those boys keep popping back up like ghosts. Something warms inside of me at the thought, and yet the sane part of me demands I lick a frozen pipe as punishment.

It's warm inside the class. It's a cozy lecture, which is what Whitney Briggs is known for—small and personalized class sizes. The chairs are set in a circle, and I go to take a seat and freeze dead in my tracks. Aiden and his dream queen sit square in front of me, holding hands, *giggling* into one another as if they were actually in love.

Oh, God.

Here it is, that two-second window I have to bolt and forget this nightmare scenario ever transpired.

Aiden looks up and does his best impression of a deer in the headlights.

Crap. This is never going to work. The world is too damn small to ever escape my heartache. I'll just have to get over him the old fashioned way, by genuinely getting involved with someone else. A rebound relationship is the least I can do to give both my heart and my vagina a fresh start.

Aiden offers up a nervous smile as I slip into my seat.

I squint over at both him and the glorified set of vocal cords, and that familiar rage percolates to life inside me.

I'm sick and tired of getting pissed off each time I see them. There has to be some way to take back the power I gave him to break my heart on a loop each time they're around. The guy to my left probably has a girlfriend he mauls every chance he gets, and that doesn't even remotely antagonize me. It's obvious I let Aiden burrow in too deep. Now I just have to figure out how to pluck him out. He's like a parasite, hard as hell to get rid of but worth the effort if you plan on living a long, productive life. I'll probably have to gouge him out of my heart with a pair of tweezers then set his ass on fire like a tick.

"Welcome, everybody, I'm Professor Novak." A small, balding man takes the lead and sits among us. "I think we all realize how lucky we are to have such a superstar in our midst—Ms. LeAnn Cleo for those of you living under a rock."

I glare over at both her and Aiden. I'd like to stone a few people right about now.

"Ms. Cleo"—he continues—"please, tell us everything you know about business, about life, about love." He laughs as he holds out a hand in acknowledgement of their blatant molestation of one another.

"Are you kidding?" She giggles into Aiden. "I would love to! But I have to warn you, I have a way of stealing the spotlight." More annoying giggles ensue, and I'm pretty sure I have a mirror I can break in my purse to cut her with. "In fact, I might just steal your class right out from under you."

"I can attest to that," I mutter.

Professor Novak lets out a little laugh of his own. "Au contraire, Ms. Cleo. I would have to be willing, in some small way, to gift it to you. It takes two to tango as they say."

I sink a little in my seat because he's right. As much as LeAnn might have seduced Aiden from me, it wasn't the first time he dipped his wick in foreign terrain. Aiden wanted her. He cheated willingly. And if I didn't think I could have my heart stomped on anymore than it already has been, then I was badly mistaken.

It was almost easier to pretend she stole him, that he was kidnapped from my bed by her ridiculous back-up singers and taken to her sound-system-enhanced lair. But that's not how it went down at all. Aiden's dick simply pointed him in another direction, and he was more than willing to follow.

Maybe it's me. Maybe I'm not likable—*lovable*. Maybe I never will be.

ഇൗരു

The pity party hits its pinnacle on Friday night when I stupidly let Cole talk me into meeting him at the Black Bear for drinks. Of course, Cole will actually be serving the cocktails in question, and I'll be required, by social etiquette, to tip him for the effort. I step in and glance around at the bevy of drunken bodies already thrashing to the death-metal blaring over the speakers—girls are jumping up on the far end of the bar unbuttoning their blouses and grinding their hips into one another.

Holt must be in charge of this three-ringed circus tonight because Bryson usually has this place on a much tighter leash.

A pair of hands cover my eyes from behind, and I jump.

I hate this game. I'm not perky enough to care who's playing peek-a-boo with me, come to think of it, peek-a-boo annoyed the hell out of me as a child. I should pretend to return the favor and not-so-accidentally take their eyes out Three Stooges style. That ought to teach them for messing with mine.

"Let go, or I'll bite." I spin, fully expecting to find Cole and that deep-dimpled grin I've secretly waited all day to see, but it's not, it's that shit-eating grin I was hoping to *never* see again—Aiden. "You have a lot of nerve." I take a step to his left, and he's quick to block my path.

"Wait." His familiar cologne wafts through the air, and suddenly choking on Drakkar Noir feels like a real possibility. And, to think, I bought him that pricey bottle. "I think we should talk."

"Go cry to LeAnn. Maybe she's interested in what you have to say."

"Chill out, would you?" His eyes squint into me as if he's genuinely annoyed. Aiden has the looks of a dark-haired Ken doll with his precision-chiseled features, those long comma like dimples that press in, those papery-blue eyes that mimic a clear stream, and now all of the things I once thought were special about him make him look like some cheesy third rate model trying to sell you a winter coat in July. LeAnn can have him, plastic balls and all.

"Look, Rox"—he grips me by the elbow and steps into me until I can smell his shitty breath—"I just want you to know that I'm thinking about asking her to marry me. Out of respect, I thought you should be the first to know."

"Out of *respect*?" I gag on the river of words trying to burst from my vocal cords. "Try not cheating on your girlfriend of three years out of respect. Or"—I dig my finger in my cheek to exemplify what a sarcastic bitch I can be—

"how about you exit one relationship before starting the next? But you wouldn't know anything about that, would you?"

I spot Cole over at the bar passing a drink to a patron through the legs of some bimbo busy twerking in his face.

"Let go." I yank my elbow free. "My boyfriend is expecting me." I scowl over at Cole for being useless at the moment. "*And*"—I turn back to the loser that I once let degrade my body—"just to be clear, I find you repulsive, Aiden. You could marry an orangutan. I couldn't care less. I hope she cheats on you twice a week for the rest of your miserable lives so you'll finally know how crappy it feels."

He yanks me back in. His lips set in a snarl. "I don't want there to be any bad blood between us. LeAnn is perfect. Look, I know you still want me. There are ways we can be together, and we'll never have to worry about money."

"Please." I glance down at his crotch like a threat. "Like I'd ever touch you again. Enjoy your sugar momma while you've got her."

I push him the hell off me.

"Yeah, and what did you get?" He calls after me. "A *bartender*? Hey, I know, maybe I'll hire him to work at my wedding!"

The riotous crowd drowns out his sorry voice as I maneuver my way to the bar.

I'm shaking. Every muscle in my body drips with adrenaline.

What a butthole.

"He's an idiot!" I say out loud, but my voice gets swallowed up in the noise from the bar.

I spot Cole serving some lush dressed in mesh from head to toe, and I shove her off the barstool and take a seat.

"Watch it, bitch." She shoulder-checks me before getting her drink and doing a disappearing act.

"Nice going." Cole cinches his lips up one side. "Because of your musical chair move, she didn't leave a tip."

I pluck a wad of twenties from my purse and stuff them in his hand. "That should make up for it. Give me a stiff one, and keep 'em coming." I growl like a tiger until he moves.

He narrows those glowing eyes onto mine. His lips twitch as if he were holding back a smile. "A stiff what?" I swear his crotch just swiveled, and I'm momentarily reminded that Cole specializes in stiff ones.

"I don't know, *genius*. I don't drink."

Holt comes over with his smug smile, his chronic bedroom eyes. "What's up, Rox?"

"What's the girly drink of the night?" I demand.

His eyes widen a notch. "Pink Panty Dropper."

Cole pumps with a dry laugh because we both know that's his personal specialty.

"Then that's what I want." I shoot a hard look to my hotter-than-hell roommate with his full lips, his I'm-going-to-put-you-to-bed-myself lustful look in his eyes. "Give me ten."

They both jerk at the idea.

"No," Holt flat lines. He smacks Cole in the stomach. "One at a time. And never get close to ten." He takes off to man the other end of the bar.

Cole plunks a small glass in front of me and pulls out two different poisons to mix up this magic potion guaranteed to make my panties flee voluntarily.

"So what's sponsoring the panty raid?" He swoops in for a moment, and the thick scent of his cologne sends a spear of excitement through me. I like how Cole smells, masculine, alive, and, most importantly, different than Aiden.

"Men suck." I glance over my shoulder and spot Laney and Baya walking in, so I flag them down.

"You're painting an entire gender with a pretty broad brush."

Baya tackle hugs me. "Who's a pretty broad?" She leans over and slaps her brother on the shoulder.

"Never you mind," I bark at him. "You just get to the business of mixing my panties a drink."

"Whose panties are drinking?" Laney looks wide-eyed and afraid.

"This girl's," I say as I snatch the pink concoction from him and sniff it. Smells like mint and piss.

"She doesn't drink." Laney says to Baya, and they exchange looks as if an intervention were needed long before my liver has the chance to shrivel up and die.

"I do tonight." I lift my glass in their direction. "Who's going to hold my hair?" When I vomit, but I leave that part out.

The music goes off in a few violent jolts before cutting away to a new song that's much more livable for my eardrums.

"Hold your hair?" Baya looks sorry for me.

I nod taking my first sip, and my face sours.

"You're lucky your brother has to work tonight, or he'd be dragging you home by the hair." Laney plucks the drink from me and takes a quick sip. "Let's dodge this little pink bullet, shall we?" She tries to pass my glass back to Cole, but I'm quick to intercept. "My sister's coming down, and we can totally make it a mission to get her laid. Won't that be fun?" She nods at me like I'm a three-year-old.

"Oh, *yes*"—my voice drips with irony—"I would love to roll your sister in honey and throw her into the beehive that just stung me. *Please*." I scowl up at Cole and his amply-endowed crotch. "I say we slaughter every human with a procreation station dangling from their bodies."

Baya shoves her balled up fists into her hips and glowers at Cole. "Nice work."

"What did I do?" He wipes down the surface of the bar in front of me, and something in his domesticated move endears me to him.

"You exist as one of them," I mutter taking my drink by the balls and carefully pouring it down my throat.

Fire. I push it away as my body gives a mean shudder. "Gah!" It rips from me like a battle cry. "What the hell is in there? Rubbing alcohol?"

"Oh, sweetie." Laney touches my cheek with her cold hand, and I only remotely feel it as my entire body goes numb.

"Shit," I whisper as my head spins like a top.

A girl walks over, bopping up and down, smiling, perky as shit, and I suddenly wish I had left a tiny reserve at the bottom of my glass so I could throw it in her exuberant little face.

"Izzy!" Laney throws her hands around her.

Izzy is Laney's sister who I think I met once, but our families don't mix much due to the fact my mother likes to put her bitch face on to anyone outside her country club, thus the slight confusion I'm having.

They lose themselves in conversation, and a sea of bodies moves between us, causing their little circle to drift toward the dance floor, and the next thing I see is the three of them thrashing their limbs to some alternative 80's music that's being covered by the world's worst singer. It sounds live....and oh, crap. Every muscle in my body freezes because I happen to recognize that mall concert, smoky-tokey voice as none other than Steal-Your-Man LeAnn.

Cole looks past me at the stage and shakes his head. "Sorry, cupcake. It's karaoke night." His dimples flex, no smile.

"That's okay." I flick my fingers at him, and he creates another Pink Panty Dropper like his life depended on it. "I had a little heart to heart with my ex at the door, and you know what I discovered?" I shout up over the music until my own voice sounds like some irritating garbage disposal.

"That you have the natural ability to verbally challenge the virility of a man?"

"Are you calling me a bitch?" I almost like him a little better now.

"No, I'm calling you *witty*. Most women would simply give him the finger. You like to add a sentimental touch he can reflect on later."

"Witty." I roll my eyes at the idea. "Second thought, next time I'll just give him the finger."

I swipe the drink from him and begin pouring it down my throat, enjoying the sting. I like pain you can feel, it's much more useful than a broken heart caused by a dumbass boyfriend. That kind of pain just kills you for no real reason other than to exemplify the fact you were an idiot to begin with.

Cole moves back and forth serving up an entire rainbow of Panty Droppers, although I'm guessing those other drinks come with fancy names of their own, like Poison for LeAnn, or Arsenic for Aiden, the Ball Buster, the Bitch Slap, the Stick Your Penis in Another Girl and Die.

I knock back the rest of the hard pink lemonade and slap my hand over the bar until Cole starts mixing me another. I fall into his midnight-colored hair with my gaze and get lost in the sea of perfection that is Cole Brighton.

"I'm going to give you a tip you won't believe." It slurs from me.

"You're going to flip my beav? Sounds dirty." He cheers me with my own glass before sliding it over. "Looking forward to it. Will it hurt?"

I try to nod, but my head feels as if it's weighted with lead as I nosedive toward the bar until my forehead comes to rest on the hard, cool granite.

"Whoa, princess. I think it's time to call it."

He reaches for my glass at the same time I secure it with a death grip, and his fingers clasp over mine.

"Yous feels *nice*." I lift up to look at him. The light shines down, illuminating him like some alien being. Cole has the face of an angel.

He closes his eyes a minute too long. "I think it's quitting time for you, sweetheart."

"I thought I was your cupcake?" The words pop from my lips like rock candy.

His cheeks flex with a grin, and my stomach spins and burns, and I swear the blue bird of happiness just flew around his head. Or was it mine?

I bat the air for a minute as I try to right myself.

Baya and Laney come back with Dizzy Izzy in tow. She looks so much like Laney I have to do a double take.

Damn, she looks good in that zebra print she's wearing. I open my mouth to tell her and yak on the floor between us with Laney catching my hair just in time.

Screaming ensues, hysteria fills the air, and that's mostly just from me.

Laney helps me off the stool and over to the bathroom.

"Spank you," I murmur.

"You wish." She growls while scratching her nails over my back. "And you're welcome."

ॐ✿

After a piping hot shower, Laney and Baya help wrap me in a robe and land my drunk ass on the sofa back at my apartment.

"I've got it from here." Cole turns on the television and flops on the opposite couch. "Nothing a little cage fighting can't cure." He turns it up a little too loud.

"I swear I will vomit on your mattress if you don't turn that shit down."

"Anything for you, cupcake." He reduces the volume until my ears stop bleeding.

"Are you sure you're feeling better?" Baya touches her cool hand to my forehead, obviously checking to see if I've contracted Pink Panty fever.

"I'm fine." I make a face because the room keeps spinning like a top, and it's taking everything in me to keep from tipping over.

"Okay, we're going to get back to the bar. I left my sister on autopilot, and she doesn't have the best sense of direction when it comes to guys."

"Sounds like we have a lot in common," I quip, hugging a throw pillow.

I give a brief wave as they take off to continue their fabulous Friday night, which I sort of put a damper on with my spontaneous puke fest.

I look over at Cole stretched out across the couch in his Levis and Black Bear T-shirt.

"You can go back," the words gravel out of me. "I'd hate for you to lose the hours. Trust me, I can conduct the remainder of this pity party on my own."

"Are you kidding? And leave all this fun? Besides, I've never been to a pity party I didn't secretly enjoy."

"I'll cure you of that." I sink into the sofa. "Anyway I'm glad to announce I'm finally over the dingleberry that hijacked my dignity."

He turns the TV down a notch and looks over. "Then what's keeping the pity party rolling?"

"Life." I lie down and prop my head on the pillow. "I can't believe I got wasted as a way to commemorate my freedom."

"Take note, you're a light weight. I hardly put a drop of alcohol in those things."

"Are you accusing me of being dramatic? You're the one who kept shoving those dirty panties in my face."

"All right, cupcake. I can see where this is going." He flexes a wry smile, and I drool just a little. "Why don't we watch something you want?" He starts flipping through the channels. "The Shopping Network? I hear they save all the best dildos for after midnight." He winks over at me.

"Takes one to know one." I'm not sure that made sense, but I'm still riding the ethanol coattails of those panty twisters.

"That it does." He gives the remote another few good flips and lands on some stale comedy from the fifties that looks as if someone colored in everyone's clothes with a crayon.

"Turn this crap. It's making me nauseated."

"Yes, ma'am." He continues to flip through at a manic rate.

"Why are you so nice to me when I'm trying my hardest to be mean to you?"

"Because, deep down, I know you're anything but mean."

I let out a groan because I'm this close to vomiting out my affection for him, literally.

Cole pulls his shirt up to his armpits and pats his chest a few times while trying to land us on something mutually edifying. He adjusts his body until his chest faces me, never taking his eyes off the screen. Damn—washboard abs, the smooth, lean strips of muscle that striate over his torso, his naturally tan skin, just the peek of a happy trail leading from his bellybutton—Cole Brighton has the body of a sex god.

"How about *The Outsiders*?"

"Only featuring every 80's star that ever lived. No thanks." I insert the tip of my finger in my mouth as I continue to drool over the long mass of muscle he's morphing into. I try to imagine myself coiled around him with those overblown biceps holding me down. I can practically feel his fingers digging into my hips.

"Here, this should do." He tosses the remote on the floor as if to prove his point.

I glance over to find The Food Network on. A man sporting a manufactured grin gives us the tour of a donut factory.

"Oh yeah, baby." Cole groans as if a couple dozen glazed donuts have the ability to get him off, and I'm guessing they do.

My eyes trace down his chest, down to his hips and stay a while just staring at his crotch like it was planning an attack. I crush my teeth over my lower lip and imagine what he might be hiding in there. Swear to God, I've never seen a bulge like that on a guy in a resting position. Aiden had the uncanny ability to look like a girl in blue jeans, and here Cole looks as if he's hoarding some kind of sexual contraband of the anaconda variety.

Cole lets out a beast of a groan, and I glance at the television in time to see the donuts falling into the glazer, resurfacing with their sugary gloss, still wet on their backs.

"Aw, fuck." Cole writhes over the sofa, and a moan of my own gets locked in my throat. "I can't take much more of this before I hop in my car and hit an all-night donut shop." He picks up the remote and turns down the volume, hoping to defuse the food porn that's gripping him by the balls, and my eyes sort of stray in that general region. Damn, by the looks of things, Cole Brighton has a supersized package. I bet he has balls the size of apples.

"Hey, cupcake"—he waves a finger in my direction—"my eyes are up here. Did you hear my question?"

"Walls?" Gah! Now there's a regretful combo of *balls* and *what*. Note to self: Never, ever drink again. In fact, stay away from all liquids just to be safe.

He frowns a moment before returning the favor and trailing his gaze from my head down to my feet.

"You painted your toes." His dimples flash in and out approvingly at my bright red polish.

"Don't look at my pigs." I tuck my legs back and readjust myself on the couch.

Cole bucks out an obnoxious laugh that makes me want to choke a litter of kittens.

"What's so funny?"

"Nothing, it's just that I hear that *I'm* a pig all the time."

"Oh, so you're a pig, too? I suppose your next line will be 'let's go make some bacon.'"

His lip twitches as he fights to hide that sarcastic as hell smile. "You wanna get cookin', good lookin'?"

"Right, like I'd ever make *bacon* with you. You're a player. Sex is nothing more than a clinical experience. The next time I share my body with someone, I want it to mean something. I want to be in love." I shake my head because we both know what a fairytale that is. True love is just as realistic as unicorns and vampires. Come to think of it, I'd prefer hanging out with a unicorn or vampire.

He narrows those thick, dark brows at me, and his eyes smolder into mine. "All right, why don't we play a drinking game? You already did the drinking so we can segue right into the fun part." He rests the remote over his granite abs, pointing downward toward the volcanic bulge that's threatening to compromise the fabric of his jeans.

"Okay, what is it?"

"*Never.*" He gives a sly grin, and my stomach pinches with heat. "Never have I kissed a nun. Your turn." He gives a slow seductive wink, and, suddenly, the alcohol has me believing I'm on the wrong couch.

"Never have I seen someone have so much sex. That would be you, by the way, you're a freak, and, no, I haven't actually witnessed your night moves. I'm relying solely on the moans and groans I've heard coming from your room. Swear to God, this place turns into a bona fide haunted whorehouse after midnight."

"I haven't had sex in weeks." He flat lines.

"Oh, poor you. Are you cramping up? Do you need me to run out to some all-night sex shop and buy you a blowup doll?"

Cole spears me with those glowing green eyes. "You'll do." His cheek rises up one side because he's too damn cocky to give into the shit-eating grin that's dying to break out on his face.

I could give him the finger or shoot off another smartass remark, but I choose to take the highroad this once.

"Back to the game," I snip. "Never..." I nestle into my pillow and consider it for a moment as my entire life unravels before my eyes. "Never did I think I'd be such a loser."

"You're not a loser." His dimples press in, and my stomach ignites like a ball of Pink Panty Dropping fire. I seriously hope that's not the puke wanting to impress me with a reprisal. "I'll go," he whispers. "Never did I think my dad would leave me."

The mood in the room shifts. Cole keeps his gaze on the television, but I can tell he's looking right through it.

"What happened to your dad?"

"He got hit by a car. He was a cyclist and died doing what he loved. Drunk driver clipped him—his helmet flipped off, hit his temple on a rock. The rest is history."

"Oh my, God. I'm so sorry." And here I was wallowing in my own misery. Poor Cole and Baya won't ever get to see their dad again. "How old were you when this happened?"

"High school." He forces a dry smile. "Anyway I probably shouldn't have went there."

"No, I'm glad you did. So, what was he like? Were you close?" I've always been fascinated with other people's parents. Especially since the relationship with mine has been like walking on eggshells.

"He was great. He had his own construction company and always bounced his ideas off Baya and me. He took us into the office a few times. It was nice. We got to see him in action."

"What's your best memory of him?"

Cole takes a breath. His chest expands, wide as a door. "He used to come into my room each night before bed, and we'd talk about the day, just us guys. He would tell me all about his glory days at WB."

"He went here?"

"Yup. He promised me college would be the time of my life."

"Is it?"

Cole blinks over with glassy eyes. "I don't know." It rasps from him gruff and, despite our topic of conversation, sexy as hell. "I thought if I threw myself at anything that moves I'd have the time of my life, that it would fill this black hole my dad left when he died, but I don't feel any different."

I take him in with his dark lashes bowed, grief imprinted on his face. I wish he wasn't hurting. That somehow I could take away the pain and make it all better, but I imagine death is an immovable stone that settles in your life that you can never get rid of.

"I know this is going to sound lame, but I can relate a little, you know, about the hole. Not in the same way you can—I mean, that's way worse. But my parents left the same hole in my heart without meaning to. I think the only time they noticed I was around was when I was baking treats for them. The whole house would smell good, and for an hour or so everyone was happy. We felt like a regular family. Then my dad would get lost in his office, and my mother would be planning some big event. Ryder would take off with his friends, and it was just me again, all alone. I guess sometimes it's nice to have someone make you feel special—to make you feel like you count."

He gives a slow nod, the look of sorrow on his face.

Then I do the unthinkable. I get up and go over, lying down next to him until our bellies touch.

"Never have I fallen asleep in the arms of someone like you." I wrap my arms around his waist and hold him, wishing all his pain away—and my pain, too.

His eyes widen, his soft, warm breath tickles my lips.

"Hey there," he whispers.

"Hey." Way to bring the awkward to the table. "I may have no real social etiquette." I bite down on my lip. "Like ever."

Cole smolders at me with those bedroom eyes. His mouth curves out with the hint of a wicked smile.

Holy hell. Clearly I've made a huge mistake. Of course, he's going to think I want to sleep with him. Isn't that exactly what I said?

"I'm not sleeping with you." It speeds out of me.

His chest thumps against mine as he fights to hold back that full blooming grin waiting to take over.

"I mean, I am." I settle my arms around him and let my body mold to his. "But not like that."

It feels good to touch him this way, platonically, of course, through several layers of clothing.

"Not like that." He repeats, but it comes out more of a question. "Like this." He runs his hands down my back and stops just shy of my hips. A chill runs up my spine like fingers gliding over the keys of a piano.

Cole presses his lips over my forehead before resting his cheek against mine.

"I think you're special, cupcake. I think you count."

I strengthen my arms around him and nestle in.

"I think you're pretty special, too, Cole."

Cole

The morning light trickles in through the curtains, and much to my surprise, Roxy is still snug in my arms as if she wanted to be here. I thought for sure once the vodka wore off she'd morph back into her lovable ball-busting self. In all honesty, there was something downright sweet about her last night, vulnerable even.

My fingers mold over her hips before skimming up the side of her body, and I dig my hand into her thick mane like I've wanted to for the last few weeks. It feels smooth, slippery, and I bury my face in it for a minute, taking in its strawberry scent. My boner ticks to life, but I don't care. I've been dying to be this close—to smell her vanilla-scented skin, taste that cherry ripe mouth. I land my lips over her temple and linger.

"What?" She groans, twisting away from me as if trying to get her bearings. "Wait, what is this?" She looks around with those sleepy eyes, and my dick rubs up against her stomach. "Oh, shit!" She spikes up. "What's going on?" Her hair is messy, her mascara smudged just enough, and it's become pretty obvious I'm going to have to slick one off in the shower just to get through the day.

"Nothing's going on, I swear." I press back into the sofa. "It's just a bathroom boner, I promise."

She snatches the pillow and covers her chest with it. "Gross." Her eyes flit down to my crotch.

"I'll take a quick shower." I get up careful not to touch her.

Roxy grazes her bottom lip with her teeth, her eyes never leaving my crotch. "I'll make us breakfast."

My heart warms just hearing her say that, and it startles me. Funny, when other girls have offered, it would make my blood run cold.

"You don't have to do that."

She gives a shy smile. "I want to."

She wants to.

I float all the way to the shower. I shake one out just to get the tension to a bearable level and change for the day before making my way back to the kitchen.

The oven is on, and the counter has been taken over with a sack of flour and a bowl full of butter. I like where this is going.

"What's for breakfast?" Actually, my stomach wanted me to rephrase that and ask *when* is breakfast. It looks like we're taking the long road to nutritional satisfaction. But I don't care as long as Roxy's the one I get to kill time with.

"What's one of your favorite foods?"

I knock my head back and think about it a minute. "Peanut butter and jelly."

"Then that's what I'm making. Peanut butter and jelly cupcakes."

"Just like that?" If I had known she was going to do whatever I asked I would have requested something far more sinfully delicious—like Roxy herself.

"Just like that. I have to be ready to cook anything and everything on the spot. The competition is coming up, and I need to be ready for anything. This will be a good experience for me."

"Sweet. In the meantime, I'll make some bacon and eggs." I pull out what I need, and within three minutes the entire apartment is lit up with the thick scent of bacon grease. I inhale a deep breath and take it all in. Roxy and bacon, now that's one heady combo.

Roxy slides open the center drawer and accidently brushes her bottom against my thigh.

"Oh, sorry." She jumps up, red-faced that we've touched.

"Not a problem."

Roxy dips her chin to her chest. Her eyes latch onto mine with a look that says she's about to eat me for breakfast, and, holy hell, I hope she does.

"Get over here." She points to her feet.

"Sure thing, cupcake." My lip curls up one side because I happen to know it's the last thing she wants me to call her, but she's cute like one and I'm guessing tasty, so I don't see me stopping anytime soon. "Hand me a fork."

I do as I'm told. "You want a hand mixer? I think I've got one around here somewhere." Mom sent a bunch of nonsensical shit when I first moved in. Not that I didn't appreciate her efforts.

"Nah, this way I get to take out all my aggressions on these poor defenseless ingredients." She smashes an egg over the lip of the bowl, and my balls shrivel.

"Whatever turns you on, cupcake."

"Why are you calling me that?" She cracks another egg, then another.

"Because a cupcake is soft inside like you." I blink a smile at her before shutting off the stove over in my arena. The eggs are scrambled to perfection, not too dry, not too slimy, and the bacon has reconfigured into crunchy curls just the way I like it.

"Yeah, well, you're going to ruin my image, so you better knock it off," she grunts it out while teaching those ingredients who's boss.

"Cupcake," I say it again as I pull out two plates. "Cupcake, cupcake, *cupcake*."

She drops the fork, and it clinks against the side of the bowl.

"Wow, Brighton, you can't go twenty-four hours without crawling onto my last nerve, can you?" She glares over at me, and I know for a fact any vulnerability that she may have displayed last night has left the building. Roxy is back, and she brought her game face to prove it. Her eyes slit to nothing. She leans against the counter with her bare foot up over the cabinet, her long, lean body flexed backward, that black waterfall of hair caressing her shoulders. Hot damn. If I didn't know better, I'd swear she were posing for me.

"Twenty-four hours?" I walk over and set the plates down as my body heats up behind her. "Is that all it's been?" I whisper directly into her ear, and she takes an audible breath.

She's got to be feeling something. I've never had such a bionic hard-on to contend with before that hasn't been reciprocated on some level. And a piece of me will fucking die if she's not feeling it. Roxy has single handedly disabled my ability to get it up for anybody else, and I'm stumped by her superpower.

I linger over her neck and take in her scent, butter and sugar, vanilla layered just beneath that. *Fuck*. Roxy smells like a cupcake, and now my lips want to try her out to verify whether or not she tastes like one, too. I'm betting yes, sweeter even.

Her breathing picks up pace. Her heart starts thumping so loud, I can hear it thundering, see it palpitating from beneath her shirt like a mini earthquake.

My lips press over her neck, soft as a feather. I dot a trail of soft kisses up the side of her cheek, slowly meandering toward her mouth. She hasn't sliced off my balls yet, so this has to be a green light.

"Are you going to molest my face all day with your lips, or are you going to kiss me?" The words come from her shaky as if she meant them as a barb, but they get lost in translation.

My lips pass over hers like the dusting of the wind, and I pull back to gauge her reaction.

Her eyelids flutter. Her lips edge forward for more, and I land my mouth square onto hers because that's exactly what I plan on giving her, more.

A groan rockets from her chest as I compress my lips hard over hers, and Roxy gives. She opens her mouth, and I fall in with my tongue sweeping over hers hungry and fierce just like those kisses back at the Black Bear, only now there isn't an audience. This is no bogus liplock drummed up in the name of some fake relationship. This is the real deal happening in real time. Roxy isn't fighting it, or manufacturing some scheme to make someone jealous. Roxy wants this kiss as bad as I do.

We're all moans and groans. Her teeth scrape against mine, and I bite down playfully over her tongue. I pick her up by the thighs and set her on the counter as she relaxes her arms over my shoulders.

Roxy slips her mouth over to my ear creating an erotic trail of heat and moisture that cools instantly in her wake.

"Fuck me," she whispers it low and husky.

The exact words my hard-on wanted to hear.

I pull back and take her in like this, hotter than a kitchen fire with her hair tousled, her eyes smoldering into mine, and I do something I hope I won't live to regret.

I say, "No."

6

Preheat

Roxy

"He said what?" Laney grips me by the wrist so hard I think she just gave me some kind of rejection-inspired fracture.

"He said *no*." I glance over at Baya as she sinks in her seat.

"That must have been awkward." She bites over her lip. "Cole has always been a great guy at heart. I'm sure there was a reasonable explanation." Baya and Bryson just came from the Witch's Cauldron, a hot spring a little north of here where apparently they exercise their coital rights quite often. I suppose having my way with Cole in nature's hot tub is off limits now that his sister's naked body has defiled the waters. I've spent all afternoon dreaming and scheming of the places and spaces I could have him.

"Oh, it was awkward," I assure. "But don't worry, he's just on his period."

Laney barks out a laugh, but Baya doesn't seem that amused.

"I jest." I kick her lightly under the table. We're outside of Hallowed Grounds freezing our asses off, while the frozen earth enjoys a gentle thaw, much like my heart. "He said we should take things slow." I take a breath just reliving the memory. "He says he's never had these kinds of feelings before, and he wants to make sure we do everything right."

"Wow." Laney's eyes bug out disbelieving. "And how hard did you hit him with the baseball bat last night?"

"Very funny." I glance over my shoulder and catch a glimpse of something horrifically familiar. A giant picture of LeAnn with her open mouth hovering over a rhinestone-studded microphone stares back at me from the student union board.

"Oh, crap," Baya moans. "It's like she's taking over campus. There's even a picture of her on the condom dispenser in the bathroom."

"We have condom dispensers in the bathroom?" I'm momentarily thrown and yet titillated by this hypersexual revelation.

"Right next to the tampons and breath mints." She affirms.

"Nice." I shake my head at the thought. "Good to know before I go and get myself knocked up by your brother," I tease.

"Speaking of knocked up"—Laney spins her coffee in her hands creating a mini plume of vapors as the heat kisses the frigid air—"the drama department is putting on *Grease*, and I'm trying out for the part of Rizzo."

"The boy crazy school girl? Sounds like type casting at its finest." I'm still pretty psyched that the boy she's crazy about is my brother. "Speaking of crazy, Aiden let me know he's thinking about asking LeAnn Cha-Ching Cleo to marry him. Also, he may have propositioned me for an affair on the side along with cash and prizes—all sponsored from the money he plans on siphoning from her account, of course."

They both gasp in turn.

Laney looks like she might be sick. "I demand you stay far, far away from that moron the next time you see him."

"Trust me, he had to pin me to the wall to have that conversation with me. We've now entered the hostage negotiations phase of our non-relationship."

"Two words: pepper spray," Baya insists.

"And brass knuckles." Laney grits it through her teeth.

"I'm carrying something better." I give a private smile. "My beating heart because he no longer owns it." I leave out the fact I think I may have given it to someone else.

Baya dips her chin and gives a knowing look. "So what's your next move with my brother?"

My cheek glides up one side as the world colors itself with the lust in my eyes.

"I'm about to prove to him that slow is overrated."

I didn't spend all morning baking peanut butter and jelly cupcakes for nothing.

A lot of things are overrated, but the way he makes my heart race sure isn't.

I'm beginning to doubt I was ever in love with Aiden at all. These butterflies, these heart-stopping jolts of desire that shoot up my thighs are all new to me.

I glance over at the snow blanketing the campus, the crowd of girls giggling to themselves, the boys tossing a football over the frozen terrain, and I'm just glad to be a part of it all.

For the first time in a long while, I don't hate the world so much.

ഔഈ

I head back home all hopped up on the idea of actually having real live sex. I haven't had "intimate relations" with anybody other than myself since early August. After a rather prolonged dry spell I figured Aiden and his wiggle worm were getting lucky elsewhere. Anyway, I let myself into the apartment, I know for a fact Cole took off for work so that gives me plenty of time to primp and pamper myself for the big naked reveal I plan on initiating later. I even went to the store and bought a half-dozen packs of cherry Kool Aid to give my hair that fiery look I love so much. And, what the hell, I might even add a few cherry-colored highlights to the runway strip I plan on fashioning out of my...

A petite blonde springs out from behind the door.

"Surprise!" She opens her coat and flashes me with an unexpected glimpse of her bits and pieces, and I accidently hit my head against the wall trying to get the hell away from her.

"Shit!" I clutch my chest for a moment. It's that girl from the bar that Cole is forever trying to get away from. "Okay, very funny, you can leave now. There's no meeting here tonight." Crap. If it's one thing Cole comes with it's some serious baggage of the psychotic female variety. Speaking of his estrogen-based carry-on, should I be worried about sexually transmitted bedbugs? Maybe I can send him a quick text. *Hi honey, would you mind running by the free clinic for me on the way home and updating your rabies shot?*

"What meeting?" The blonde ditz looks genuinely worried for a minute.

"You know"—I plop a shit ton of groceries on the counter because I bought out the store for the decadent midnight snack I plan on preparing—"the itty bitty titty committee." I shoot her a look that reeks of no mercy. "Go on, get gone. Your services are no longer required. If you don't mind, I have a girl's night planned that involves a very sharp razor and a rom com."

"I love romantic comedies." She swoons for a moment. Her tiny, tic tac shaped teeth clatter over one another, and for a second I think maybe she's mistaken it for a meal.

"Here." I hand her a peanut butter and jelly cupcake that somehow managed to escape Cole's oral assault this morning. If I'm anything, I'm about feeding people. Not to mention her boobs are in need of some stuffing.

"Thanks." She peels back the wrapper and takes a bite. "God, this tastes like heaven!"

"I know." I'm a sucker for someone who might even remotely enjoy my cupcakes. I blame my parents for that, mostly my mother. Not that she doesn't like me, she's simply mistaken me as some crisis project gone awry. She's since replaced me with her longtime assistant Meg who's been stalking my brother Ryder for the better half of a decade. I recognize a stalker when I see one and it just so happens I'm staring at one right this minute. "I think this is the part when you scat back to your sorority."

"Can't." She cinches her trench coat, and my eyes are forever grateful. "My roommate is having a guest over. Melanie is a senior, so what she says goes." She spins a finger through the air as if to say big whoop.

"Melanie Harrison?" The self-proclaimed cupcake queen of Whitney Briggs? The very Melanie Harrison who thinks she's going to pull a miracle out of her ass at the Sticky Quickie baking competition? "You know—maybe you *could* join me for that rom com."

What better time to dish about our respective roommates.

I hand her another cupcake, and she eagerly accepts.

Melanie Harrison and her Ecstasy Delights are going down.

Cole

The barflys were coming on strong with their lingering cleavage, their open-mouth pouts, but I held strong and ignored their advances. This is new terrain for me. It's sort of strange working behind the bar, observing the crowd, wondering how many of them, if not all, I've slept with. I wonder what my dad would think about that.

For so long I was open to anyone and anything, and, often times, that came with just about everything. But the thought of living that life forever, living it *again* makes my stomach twist. It's empty, always was. As soon as Roxy set up shop in the apartment, I knew there was something better, and, ironically, she was right here under my nose.

It's ten after midnight. Bryson let me off early, and, judging by the silly grin on my sister's face, I'm betting she had something to do with it. I take my tips and pick up Chinese for Roxy and me. I even paid a little extra to buy one of the candles in a jar from off their table.

I think tonight will be a great time to lay the foundation for us. I've never had a bona fide relationship before, so I'm not really sure where to start, not to mention the fact my stomach has been turning like a concrete mixer for the better half of the day because the last thing I want to do is fuck this up.

I give a gentle knock on the apartment door before opening it. The glow from the television fills the room with a soft blue haze, and the scent of something fresh baked fills the air.

"Holy hell," I whisper, taking in the heavenly scent. Both my stomach and my dick want to know how I got lucky enough to land a girl like Roxy.

I step inside and freeze. Her hair is piled on top of her head with a silver seam of metal running through it.

"Shit!"

Roxy sits on the couch, staring at the television with a...*knife* sticking out of her skull. Blood drips down the sides of her face in long, crimson tracks.

"What the hell?" I jump back.

"Cole?" My name comes from behind, and I give a slow turn suddenly rethinking my stance on personal weaponry and self-defense.

Angel stands wrapped in a trench coat, holding a plate of fresh-baked cookies.

"Get out!" I yell so loud, the cookies go flying. "You fucking *killed* her!" I roar as she runs screaming out into the hall.

A gentle laugh comes from the couch, and I turn to find Roxy wiping her face clean with a towel.

"That's one way to get rid of her." Roxy bats those long lashes up at me, and my dick perks to life despite the morbid exit wound sitting on top of her head. "But I'm hardly dead." She plucks out the butter knife, and her hair falls in one long wet wave. "Relax, I'm dying my hair." She springs to her feet and lands a lingering kiss over my lips. "Let me rinse this stuff out." Her hand trails down my back until she rounds over my ass, and I don't protest the idea. "Then maybe we can catch up on the day." She offers up a firm squeeze.

"Catch up on the day," I repeat like a moron.

I have a feeling going slow will be harder than I thought.

While Roxy showers, I move the coffee table and set up a place for our midnight picnic right here in the living room. I scan the TV until I stumble on an easy-going music channel, complete with the video of a crackling fire. What says romance more than an automated fireplace and a bowl of Kung Pao Chicken?

The bathroom door opens, and I'm quick to light the candle and set it in the middle of the blanket.

Roxy struts back, the scent of cinnamon and vanilla seep out before her.

"Wow," she muses.

I look up, and my heart stops in my chest. I'm not sure what I was expecting. Roxy usually walks around in sweats, dark Goth-like clothes that leave her figure completely up to my imagination, but this...

"Wow," is the only comeback I can think of myself.

"I'm impressed." She saunters over in her low cut, black lace dress that barely has the hemline to cover the curve of her bottom. Roxy Capwell is for all practical purposes naked, and I wholeheartedly approve—mostly.

"This is going to make going slow very *very* hard"—I lean back on my hands taking her in from head to foot—"not to mention it's having the same effect on the part of me that's trying to rip its way out of my boxers. I think, for now, we should stick to first base." Seriously? I think I'll sucker punch Bryson next time I see him for planting the idea in my head.

"Oh?" She pinches her hips. "Is this what's got you all worked up?" She tilts her head as she comes in close. "I was just getting comfortable before bed. I usually sleep naked. I was just trying to be respectful and put a little something on. I'd hate to cause a scene." Rox drops to her knees in front of me. She runs her finger from my jawline to my chest in one smooth stroke.

"Back to slow"—I run my eyes up and down her body, her peach nipples protruding through the lace—"what's going on?" I never was one for guessing games, but I'm pretty sure I can guess where she'd like this to go.

"You only have a semester left under your belt before graduation." She straddles me on either side of my hips, and I get the feeling that quick bite I snuck on my way home is all the Chinese food I'll get tonight. Not that I care. I sort of like where Roxy's head is at—skipping straight to dessert.

"Hey, cupcake." I slide her off and scoot back a good foot to put some clearance between my hard-on and the fact she's not wearing any underwear. "Just out of curiosity, you and Angel weren't playing any drinking games tonight were you?"

"Nope." She bounces over to my lap again with her hair glowing a gentle cherry red. "The only game I want to play is right here with you." Roxy's lips part seductively, and I can feel myself magnetizing toward her mouth, demanding to fall in.

"That's the thing"—I move the candle to the coffee table before we set the entire building on fire—"I think maybe we should be more than a game. I've played my fair share of games, and they all end the same way"—I pause to take her in—"with no winner."

Her eyes widen and reflect the flames from the television. Roxy is on fire, both inside and out. I've never seen a woman look so damn beautiful.

Her features harden. Her shoulders sag as she rolls off onto the carpet. "Are you giving me the I-just-want-to-be friends speech?" She folds her arms across her chest, pissed as hell. Something about the way her emotions run from one extreme to the other adds to her charm.

"No." I pick up her hand and bring it to my lips. "I'm giving you the let's-have-dinner-and-find-out-a-little-more-about-each-other speech. What makes you such a lean, mean baking machine?" I pluck all the little white boxes out of the bag and load up our plates before she morphs into a sex kitten again. Who am I kidding? Roxy has been a sex kitten right from the beginning. "What makes you tick?" Like a bomb, but I leave that part out.

"Okay." She snatches a fork and holds it up to me like a peace offering before taking a bite of her food. "Mmm, how did you know I was starving?"

"For one, you live off cupcakes. It's the only thing I've seen you eat since you've been here."

"You complaining?"

"Nope." I hold up my hands.

"Okay." She grinds her hips into the carpet, and my dick tries to tear its way out of my jeans in order to strangle me and my stupid *slow* plan of action. "You first. How old are you?"

"What?"

"You know, what year were you born? How long have you been trying God's patience?"

"Twenty-two years too long." I scoot in close. "Now it's your turn. Start from the beginning. Did you have a womb with a view?"

"Funny." She scowls to prove her point then her features soften. "When I was little, my parents were gone a lot. As soon as I was able to walk, my grandmother had me baking cookies with her." She picks at a loose thread and a smile plays on her lips. "Anyway, when I was about twelve she passed away." Her smile dissipates with the memory, and my heart breaks for her. "I still have the wooden spoon we would use. It belonged to *her* mother, and now it's mine."

"Is that?" I point over toward the kitchen at the wooden spoon hanging from the wall and try to forget the fact I offered to spank her with it.

"Yup, that's the one." She loosens with a gentle laugh. "Anyway"—she hitches her hair behind her ear like a reflex—"After Granny died, I continued to bake. I saw how happy Ryder was, so I kept doing it."

"I bet he was happy. I would have been more than enthused if Baya didn't burn the toast each time she tried to do something in the kitchen."

"I like Baya." She wrinkles her nose.

It tears me up to hear about her childhood. Her parents sound like a head-trip—a financially stable head-trip—but, then again, money has a way of magnifying flaws.

"So what about your parents? I bet they were pretty stoked to have dessert on demand." There. Nothing kills a hard-on faster than talking about someone's mother.

"That thrill only lasted for about five minutes. My dad is sort of a hard ass, and my mother thinks I'm a degenerate. They made it a sport of ignoring me and my brother when we were little. Basically they've cut me off from their money although that hasn't stopped my mother from trying to mold me into a younger version of herself. Nevertheless, my baking skills and good looks will have to get me through life. Dad was always off on business, and my mother was too busy trying to control society. She's the reason Ryder voluntarily removed himself from the family."

"No kidding?" I tuck my head back. I wouldn't have guessed there was any strife in the Capwell clan. I did a little internet research, and her father's company is in the Fortune 500, not that I care. I'd like Roxy if her parents were homeless.

"She's been anti-Laney from the beginning. I guess she's not the right pedigree. Social standing is more valuable than anything, including her children. My mother's judgmental that way. But I guess that's the pot calling the kettle black because I basically hate society no matter what pedigree they are."

"Sorry to hear that." Great. Now I've just depressed the hell out of both of us, not to mention the fact I'm pretty sure I won't cut the mustard with dear old Mom. "So what makes you hate people?"

"What's not to hate? Society is generally corrupt and greedy as hell."

"In bed or financially?"

"Both."

Usually this would be a segue into the bedroom for me, but something tells me Roxy's not in the mood for any of my one-liners tonight or any other night.

"What else interests you? You know, outside the kitchen."

"I like running, only now the ground is too slick to even think of it. I saw your skateboard." She nods to the corner. "I ride."

"Really?"

"Yeah, really. What's the matter? A girl can't ride a skateboard in your world?"

"Sure she can. And she's twice as hot if she does." No joke. I think every cell in my body just picketed my dinner proposition. My ears pulsate with adrenaline and swear to God they're chanting *dessert, dessert.*

"Okay." She glides in close. "Tell me something about your family. I mean I know about Baya, and you've told me some things about your parents, but I want more."

"More?" I lie back and stare up at the ceiling. "It's funny, I was just thinking about my dad today. What his thoughts would be on some of the lifestyle choices I've made, and if he would regret the grocery-store analogy."

She gives a little laugh. "I think overall he'd be happy with what he sees."

"I'd like to think so."

"So give it, Brighton. Tell me what you liked best about your old man."

"We used to do everything together. He taught me how to surf, and we'd go out on the water just about every morning." I swallow hard. "I thought it was pretty cool the way he could make something from nothing. He was like this magician. You know, an empty lot one day, and before you know it, he'd have a house or a building framed out. It was pretty incredible to witness." I reach over and interlace our fingers as if it were the most natural thing in the world. "He knew everything. You could ask him the most random question, and he would have an answer, and, of course, he'd be right. The night he went out"—my voice breaks, and I clear my throat—"I was in my room, and he said he'd be right back, so I didn't even bother with goodbye." My shoulders sink at the thought. Every day I regret not getting my ass out of bed and taking one last look at him. "I didn't think he'd hear me from my room. About ten o'clock my mom started freaking out then an hour after that, the police showed up. It was pretty much the entry to the shit factory. Baya was a mess. My mom was out of her mind. Before I knew it, she had us packed and moving to Texas. It was a suck fest all around."

Roxy reaches over and runs her fingers through my hair. "I'm so sorry." A single tear rolls down her cheek.

"Yeah, well, nothing we can do about that now."

"Sounds like you had a lot of love in your house."

"We did—still do. Mom asked me to step in and help look out for Baya." All those memories of last semester

145

come flooding back. "The fact I made Baya and Bryson sneak around makes my stomach turn. But they're together now, and she's happy—that makes me happy." I scoot in and rest my hand over her hip. I can't remember the last time I had an honest-to-God conversation with a girl, and it feels great. "Tell me about your future. What comes next after Briggs?"

"Okay, don't laugh." Her lips curl on one side, and she looks adorable as hell. "I want to open a bakery—just cupcakes at first. It's sort of my specialty."

"What do you want to call it?"

"Sprinkles Cupcakes. I can picture it in my mind, mint green walls with pink and yellow dots scattered around. It's stupid, I know. Laugh and I'll cut you."

"It's not stupid. Sounds delicious." I lean in and land a soft kiss over her lips. "I plan on being your first customer."

"Really?" Her eyes glisten with moisture.

"Yes, really. And, if I have my way, I'll build it for you, too."

"So, is that what you're going to do?"

"That's it. Construction."

"I guess that's what we have in common. We both like to create."

We're both hurting, too, but I leave that part out.

"So what exactly does 'taking it slow' mean?" She runs her finger over my stubble.

"Hell, if I know."

Roxy scoots in, and my entire damn body starts to shake. I can't take much more of this—her little black dress, that dark triangle between her legs that's been playing peek-a-boo with me for the better part of an hour—her achingly soft lips that I'm dying to cover with mine, so I go for it.

I offer a gentle peck and pull back because I'm pretty sure slow doesn't dictate jamming my tongue down her throat the way I want to, but right about now I'd die for a taste—any part of her will do, but, damn it all to hell if I'm not eyeing that triangle again.

Roxy sways her head as a light moan escapes her. Her eyes are glazed over with a lustful look that's just this side of feverish. Her mouth covers mine, and I don't fight it. I'm in, and Roxy can have me any way she wants. We're all tongues and teeth, heated breaths, and groans for a small eternity.

Roxy finally curls into me until we're spooning right there on the floor.

"I'm sleeping with you whether you like it or not," she purrs.

I wrap my arms around her because I happen to like it a hell of a lot.

7

Fail to Rise

Roxy

A dull knock thumps against the door, rousing me from a blissful dream where I'm floating on a surfboard with Cole's arms around my waist. I'm having such a great time, I'm laughing my head off.

The thumping continues, and both Cole and I let out a simultaneous groan.

"You'd better get it," he gravels it out.

"I think you'd better get it. I'm half naked, remember?"

"I like you half naked." He leans up over me and gives his signature sexy grin, all for me.

More thumping ensues. It's obvious they've moved beyond polite to pissed.

"I dreamed we were surfing." I wrap my finger around his inky, dark hair. "I want you to teach me."

His eyes widen with surprise. "Done." Cole dips a quick kiss over my lips before jumping to his feet and opening the door.

"Who are *you*?" An all-too-familiar female voice shrills through the air. "Roseanna?" Mom bursts in like a hurricane, and I scramble to cover myself with the blanket beneath me.

The Chinese boxes go flying. Rice and Kung Pao Chicken rain through the air all over her patent leather Prada shoes.

"Holy mother of God!" She lances the silence with her horror. "Are you naked?"

"No!" I wave my hand as if I were trying to stop a runaway train. "I'm totally covered." I flash her a quick glimpse of my black lace dress, and she cringes.

"Lingerie?" She gags a little when she says it. "Tell the boy to leave." She shields herself with her hand, not that it's necessary considering Cole is fully dressed. I'm pretty sure I've never been so glad not to have had sex in all my life. God knows what my mother would do if she found us both naked.

"I'll go to my room," Cole says it low, and I close my eyes because I'm pretty sure I haven't told my mother about—

"His *room*?" Her clear green eyes bug out until they look like marbles. "Oh, Roseanna." She bows her head a moment.

"Cole, it's fine, come here." I wave him over, and he slinks back reluctant. "This is my mother, Rue. Mom, this is my roommate." I swallow hard and give Cole a nervous smile because I've never said what I'm about to say next. "And my *boyfriend*, Cole." Not that Cole and I have crossed that bridge yet, but I don't see why not since Mom, here, is already having a myocardial infarction. Why not make it official?

A guttural groan emits from her as if her fingernails were being plucked out one by one.

"Please tell Cole I'd like a word with you alone." She massages her eyelids as if she were battling a migraine, and I bet she is.

"He's standing right here. You can tell him yourself." I glance to Cole, embarrassed he gets to witness my mother's lunacy firsthand.

"I'd rather not." She does a circular walkthrough of the kitchen.

Cole leans in. "I'll give you two a sec." He gives Mom a slight wave. "Nice meeting you."

"He's not the one for you." Mom's eyes sharpen over mine, and my blood boils because, for one, Cole has barely left the room.

"How would you know he's not the one for me? You don't even *know* me."

She sucks in a breath. Her black wool coat drapes to the floor, and her peach power suit peeks from beneath, giving it a Halloween effect.

"I know you full well." She tips her chin while slapping her leather driving gloves over her palm. "I came by to put in an order for the Valentine's benefit."

"Really?" I give a little hop, momentarily forgetting all the bullshit that just transpired. "That would be amazing! Business has been picking up slowly, but something this big would be the break I need. What are you thinking? Chocolate? Vanilla? Red Velvet! Or I can do a variety and have all these cute Valentine-themed decorations. Oh my, God, I can't believe this is happening to me." I slap my hand over my forehead because it all feels too good to be true, first I have a decent guy in my life for once, and now this?

She crimps her lips. "Compose yourself. It's not happening. I'm revoking the offer unless you move out of this den of perversion and distance yourself from that boy. August Johnson has a son five years your senior who just graduated law school—"

"Get out," I say it low at first with my voice shaking, my muscles trembling.

Her eyes sharpen in on mine. "What did you just say to me?"

"I said, get *out*." I can feel that suit of armor strapping itself to my back, flexing over my chest like a seatbelt. "I don't need to do the Valentine's benefit."

She blinks back as if she were genuinely surprised. "You yourself said it would change everything."

"It doesn't change you. I'm not interested in your terms, so you can go now. I'm not interested in August Johnson's son either. Cole is the best person in the world for me because, for one, he believes in me. He has faith in my business and in me as a person."

"Of course, he does." She walks abruptly toward the exit. "He sees you as his ticket out of this dump. We'll need about sixteen dozen cupcakes should you change your mind." She dusts her judgmental gaze around the apartment and smirks. "Something tells me you will."

Crap.

Why couldn't she just give me the Valentine's benefit without any strings?

Cole comes out of the bedroom with that is-the-coast-clear look on his sexy face, and I open my arms.

"Can I ask what happened?"

"I chose you."

I land my lips over his and pour out all of my affection for him as the room, Whitney Briggs, and all of the drama that goes along with it—my mother—they all disappear.

೮೨೦೪೫

A week sweeps by with Cole treating me to dinner, *making* me dinner, helping me create new combinations for my cupcake catering business.

"You should make a flyer with all the unique flavors you have to offer." He winces at an oncoming car as we wind our way down the side of the mountain.

Cole has the night off, so he offered to take me to a beach he likes to visit when he's clearing his mind.

"That's a great idea. Maybe you can help me with that."

"Already on it." He reaches over and warms my knee with his hand. "I found some cool graphics you can check out and see if you like."

"That's what I like best about you, you're always willing to pitch in. Speaking of pitching in, I wanted to ask if you'd be willing to help with the baking competition. It's just a couple of weeks away, and I'm down a body—Laney has the chance of a lifetime audition in L.A., and she can't miss it."

"I'd love to." His brows tweak as the moon pours in through the windshield and washes his skin a blue alabaster. "I'd do anything to make your dreams come true."

My heart thumps in my chest. I don't think I've ever wanted anybody as much as I want Cole Brighton.

"That's what you do for the one's you care about"—he steals a quick glance—"you support them."

My face fills with heat at the thought of anyone caring about me. I don't think I've felt this much affection, this much love, since my grandmother passed away.

Cole pulls off the highway and takes the road down to the dunes where we meet up with a giant sign that reads, *closed to public.*

I wash my gaze over his features. His stubble has grown in, and his dark hair has blue streaks throughout from the night shadows. I don't know about Cole, but my feelings have multiplied in such a short time, I'm almost afraid for myself. In all those years I was with Aiden, I thought I was in love. But compared to what I feel now, for Cole, I'm wondering if I ever even *liked* Aiden.

I give a little laugh.

"What's so funny?"

I bite down on my lip. I'm pretty sure bringing up ex-boyfriends, no matter how douchy they are, is bound to set the evening on a shitty trajectory.

"Nothing."

"It's something." He parks on the overlook, and we watch as the Atlantic Ocean washes and wanes under a pearlescent moon.

"God, this is gorgeous." We unbuckle ourselves, leaning to take in the view.

"I think you're gorgeous." He slides over, and I meet him in the middle. The heady scent of musk emanates from him, intoxicating me to the brink of sexual deprivation.

"And I think *you're* cute." I hedge in ever so close, trying to control my breathing. Cole Brighton is hotter than a grease fire, and he has my body shivering and quivering in all the right places. My mouth goes in for the kill, and I bite his lower lip playfully. Cole has kept true to his first-base policy all damn week, and I'm aching for some relief. Oh, hell, sometimes if you want something you need to go out and get it.

I pull him into a pressured kiss, swinging my leg over his hips until I'm straddling him with my knees.

Shit. I chose a crap night to wear the tightest yoga pants known to man, constructed from way more spandex than should ever be legal. I feel like a stuffed sausage in these—not to mention the fact they're sticking to my thighs, thick as sealskin.

He gives a hard moan, and I take it as a green light. My fingers pull off his sweatshirt, and I run my hands over his smooth, rock-solid chest.

"God, I'm going to roll my naked body all over this piece of art tonight." I run my tongue up to his ear and spin a little circle in it until he shudders beneath me.

"What happened to taking it slow?" He rumbles with a dry laugh because I think we both know *slow* is reserved for the chess club and virgins.

"I think we're about to get really good at baseball."

"We just glided by first." He pulls me in by the back of the neck, and his tongue goes off in my mouth like a hungry river snake. Cole runs his warm hands up the back of my sweater, inching his way toward second base.

And that's exactly when I remember I'm wearing a sports bra.

Gah! I'm so freaking *stupid*. He's going to think I have a uniboob, or worse that he's encountered the flatlands of Hollow Brook County. God knows the only thing this contraption is made to do is shrink and compress. It's the equivalent of dousing his penis with ice water—neither fair nor flattering.

"Second." He pulls back and gives the hint of a wicked grin, his eyes hardly slit open. His fingers clasp over the girls, well, the spandex that's currently holding the girls hostage, and he closes his eyes.

"Shit," he seethes, sucking in a breath through his teeth. "You're so fucking soft."

And well supported, but, thankfully, Cole has decided to let my spandex sins slide.

"Um, so what's third?" I ask trying to defuse my budding anger over the fact I chose to dress head to toe in workout gear on a *date*.

"Anything you want it to be."

I pepper kisses over his face while my fingers run wild through his hair. That's the first thing I noticed about Cole Brighton, his jet-black glossy hair. Swear to God, I'm going to run my feet through it one day, and, if it didn't require some serious contortion, I'd do it right now.

My fingers work spastically to unbutton his jeans. I bounce back to gain clearance for the boxer raid that's about to take place and accidently honk the horn with my ass.

"Excuse you." He pumps a quick smile.

"Not funny." Way to pull us out of the moment. It's like my yoga pants are out to get me. "Shut up and fuck me."

"God, I love it when you talk to me that way."

"Close your mouth and do it." I take a mean bite out of his ear, and he lets out a roar.

"Yeah, that." A dull laugh thumps through his chest. "Guess what, cupcake?" He spikes his hands into the back of my yoga pants, and a few stitches snap in his wake. It sounds like a series of mini firecrackers are going off in my crotch. "Sorry."

"I'm burning the demon-wear as soon as we get home." I run my tongue over his lips. "You were saying?"

"Mmm..." He moans right over my mouth. "I plan on inflicting a little pain of my own, starting with your—"

A beam of light flashes right at us followed by a volatile knock.

"Police! Open up."

Crap.

Let me guess, I butt dialed 911.

Cole

My fingers clench over the steering wheel as I white knuckle us all the way back to Whitney Briggs. I've gone twenty miles over the speed limit all the way home, and I'm shocked that not one of Hollow Brook's finest bothered to pull me over.

"It's going to be so much better back at the apartment, anyway," Roxy laments as I glide into my favorite parking spot and run over to open her door. "I probably would have thrown out your back with all the things I was planning to do to you."

We walk briskly through the damp night air as our breath crystalizes around us in a plume of smoke.

"Hot damn." I'm all about releasing some primal urges. My blood supply happens to be traveling south at the moment, so I'm a little short on words. I haven't had sex in weeks. My balls ache just thinking about it. But tonight isn't about sex, and everything in me knows it.

I pull her in by the waist, and we land under the lamppost with its spray of light illuminating the mist like a million dancing particles.

She hops up on my hips, and I grip her under the thighs.

"I just thought of something," I whisper.

"That you'd rather I ride you in the parking lot?" She attacks me with her tongue, and I laugh with her right there in my mouth. Something tells me Roxy Capwell is going to be a wild vixen in bed, and not one ounce of me is complaining.

"No." I pull back and take her in with her dark hair, her porcelain smooth features, her lips full and throbbing. I take a breath. "I just..." a part of me doesn't want to fess up. I'm afraid maybe it's the bad boy in me that's supercharging her batteries, and I'm half afraid to wipe off that sheen. Then I launch right in, no holds barred. "I just realized that I've never been so turned on, so physically excited, so outrageously ready to explode." I touch my nose to hers a moment and close my eyes. "I guess in a way it sort of feels like the first time." Nice. Why don't I tell her I have a secret vagina she can scout out later, too?

"Cole," my name whispers from her lips. Her features soften. She's letting down her armor, and it only makes me want her that much more. "I feel the exact same way."

Great. Now that we've established we're at the like-a-virgin phase of our relationship, maybe we should go for broke, or at least I should.

"I think I'm in love with you." Everything in me loosens. It's as if I've been holding up a five hundred pound weight over my head these last few weeks, and getting those words out is the only way to feel some relief.

Her eyes sparkle with tears, and she's quick to blink them away.

"I *know* I'm in love with you, Cole Brighton." She lands those luscious lips over mine, and I walk us backward into the apartment building with my heart soaring right out of my chest. This is incredible—something that I would have never believed was possible unless I experienced it myself, and am I ever glad I'm experiencing it myself.

I bump into a body, and someone yells, *get a room* as they head outside.

Rox and I share a laugh without ever moving away from the magical kiss we're locked in.

It takes everything in me not to have my way with her in the elevator. Her legs lock tight around my waist until she's rising above me, climbing me like a pole—our lips never breaking contact.

We stumble out into the hall, and I get us to the door.

I fumble with the key and spin Roxy as we crash into the apartment with a bang.

I'm ready to haul her to the couch and freeze.

Baya and Bryson sit on one sofa, Laney and Ryder on the other.

Roxy and I look at each other before she engages in a rather unceremonious dismount.

"Look who's here?" She scratches at the back of her hair, and her cleavage ripples from the low V in her sweater amping me up that much more. It's becoming apparent that my hard-on gives a rat's ass that a peanut gallery suddenly morphed into our living room. The train has already pulled out of the station. It's go-time whether or not anyone tries to stop it.

"Pipe burst in our bathroom." Baya shrugs apologetically. "They said it might take a couple days to fix it. The carpet is ruined."

"You mind if we crash?" Bryson gives me a look that says *dude, so sorry for your boner.*

"Not a problem." I've had plenty of sex with people in the next room. I'm a pig that way, but something in me doesn't want my first time with Rox to be like that.

Her brother shoots me a look that says *your balls are going to die.* "Looks like I might need to crash, too." He looks from me to Roxy.

Shit. I know all about the big brother baseball bat he's ready to beat me down with.

"It's not like that," I say in a lame attempt to defuse his temper, but we both know it's exactly like that.

He jumps up and knocks his chest into mine before slamming me to the wall.

"You think I'm an idiot?" He spins me around and bashes my face into the door jam. "Explain these marks to me. In fact, why don't you tell the whole damn room what they mean, and look at my sister while you do it!" He turns to her. "Which row do you want to be on, Rox? Because that's all you'll ever be to him is another notch on his wall.

Is that what you want?" His voice echoes around the room like a boomerang.

"Hey"—Bryson plucks him off me—"chill out, would you?"

"Don't tell me to chill out." He struggles free from Bryson's grasp. "If this were Annie, you'd react the same way."

Bryson shoots me a look that says he's right. Bryson's kid sister is a senior in high school, and something tells me both he and Holt will burn off any idiot's penis with a magnifying glass if they try to get it anywhere near Annie.

"Look, I'm not a monster." I hold up my hands.

Roxy comes over and wraps an arm around my waist. "He's not, Ryder, so you can put away your testosterone and take it down a notch. Did I ever once give you crap about who you dated? *No*." She roars in his face, and he blinks. "I supported you! You're the only person in our family I thought I could count on to have my back. Well I guess I was wrong." She steps in close. "And, by the way"— she sneers into him—"I'll be sleeping in my own room while Baya and Bryson are here, so you can put away the chastity belt. But after that"—her lips curl, taunting him in the process—"where and with whom I choose to sleep is my business."

Roxy heads into her bedroom and slams the door.

"Nice work, moron," I say before heading for the hall and Ryder pulls me back with a violent yank. "Look, I happen to really care about your sister."

He glances at the scoreboard. "I see how you *care* about girls. The only moron in this room is you. Keep it in your pants because if I find out you took advantage of her, I'm going to break some bones."

I glare at him a moment. I should shake his hand, tell him it's cool, assure him that I would never hurt his sister, but I'm too pissed over the fact he just threatened to snap my limbs in my own damn apartment to do any of those things.

Instead I launch my fist over his jaw and send him crashing to the floor.

Maybe he'll think twice before he threatens me again.

I head off to my room.

Alone.

8

Pour Some Sugar on Me

Roxy

Four days.

No sooner do Baya and Bryson take off than I get the biggest order of my life.

"One thousand chocolate banana cupcakes for an annual event down at the homeless shelter!" I jump up on Cole's lap, and he twirls me around the room.

"That's amazing!" He beams that dimpled grin, and I'm spellbound for a moment.

"Crap." I slink off him. "Tonight was going to be our special night, and now I'll be baking nonstop. The benefit is in two days."

"Are they paying you?"

"Enough to make my bank account sing. I'm embarrassed they've offered to pay so much, but I'm all too familiar with how these fundraisers work. There's usually someone like my mother fronting the funds for the catering, so I don't feel too bad."

"Good. I don't want you to feel bad." Cole bears into me. "And don't worry about us—we're a team. I'll even help you knock them out if you want."

"Yes!" I squeal again because it feels so good to have someone on my side. For so long it felt as though life was something hard I had to do all by myself, and now, with Cole, it feels light because he doesn't mind sharing the load and encouraging me along the way. "You know what? You're ruining me." I pinch his earlobe playfully.

"Ruining you, huh?" He rounds his hand over my bottom. "I haven't begun to ruin you." He lands a searing kiss off my lips.

Cole Brighton hasn't even begun to ruin me, and it's about the sweetest thing that anyone has ever said to me.

"I mean that in a good way. I'm not so angry at the world anymore. You've softened me." I say that last part under my breath because I'm still not so sure it's a good thing.

"You were always soft." He plants a gentle kiss over my lips. "It was the world that was trying to harden you."

Cole rakes his mouth over my cheek, and my eyes close as soon as I feel his heated breath. His lips find mine, and we fall into a kiss that stretches out far longer than I can ever afford with a thousand cupcakes on the line, but, damn it all to hell, Cole Brighton is resuscitating my soul one beautiful kiss at a time. There's not a whole lot more I can ask for.

For the next day and a half, Cole and I envelop ourselves in a cloud of flour. We run around buying entire carts full of ingredients, additional boxes we'll need for delivery, and a few more mixing bowls.

Baya offered to help, in addition to lending us her oven, so we could bake twice as fast. Of course, I took advantage of the situation and taught both Cole and Baya to masterfully frost a cupcake and all the while trying desperately not to gross her out with the sexual innuendo begging to stream from my lips.

At the end of two long grueling days, Cole helps me load up the back of his truck with all the cupcakes we worked so hard on.

I wipe my brow. "It smells like a banana factory blew up in here."

"Last I heard they were still growing them on trees, but, compared to the stink I usually have going on in here, it's an improvement."

"See? I'm losing brain cells due to lack of sleep." Cole and I haven't even shared two kisses since operation lose-my-ever-loving-cupcake-mind came into play. "I'm just glad it's over."

My cell goes off. "It's a text from the Morris Foundation."

"What's it say?" He takes the turn to downtown Jepson gingerly so the boxes don't slosh around in the back.

"Oh my, God." I just stare at my phone in disbelief. "I think I'm delirious. It says they would like to order a *thousand* cupcakes for an event they're hosting this Saturday afternoon."

"You're on fire, girl." Cole reaches over and tweaks my rib. "Do it. I'll be right there with you."

My heart warms just hearing him say it.

"I can't thank you enough for that." I take him in as the fading sunlight catches him just right with his dark hair slicked back, his glowing eyes. "I mean I know how I'd *like* to thank you." If every muscle in my body didn't ache. I'd really like to impress him with a couple acrobatics for our first time and not lie there like a limp rag.

He pats my knee as we park in front of the homeless shelter with their line snaking around the block.

"Would you look at this?" He gives a quick grimace. "You're really going to make a lot of people happy today, you know that? And I'm one of them. I'm honored to be a small part of this. Don't worry about us, Rox. As soon as we fill that next order, we'll do something special. Maybe I'll take the day off Sunday and we can see where the wind takes us." He sweeps his soft gaze over me, his finger softly touching my cheek. "I'm in this for the long haul."

I swallow down the sudden urge to cry. It looks like baking twenty-four seven, and no sex turns me into an emotional pussy.

I give a little smile. "I wouldn't want anyone else with me for the long haul but you."

We share a simple kiss before getting back to work.

⸒⸓

Both Cole and I bake our asses off. One thousand lemon raspberry cupcakes signed sealed and delivered to the Morris Foundation bright and early Saturday morning. Cole and I took two days off school just to finish on time, and poor Baya missed a class, herself.

"I don't think I should fill orders like that anymore." I tell Laney as we hunch over our coffee inside Hallowed Grounds. Cole left for work, and I'm here hoping to catch a second wind by infusing myself with caffeine.

"I think you're pretty lucky you're getting orders like that." Laney's eyes bug out. "I've never heard of anything like it. I bet your mom put in a good word to all her big wig foundation friends." She wrinkles her nose. "You know, sort of like a peace offering."

"Peace offering? My mother doesn't know the meaning." True story.

"I don't know about that—she's reached out to Ryder a few times since Christmas."

"Get out." I lean in like it's the most outrageous thing I've heard. Ryder made the decision to cut my mother out of his life because she deliberately tried to sabotage his relationship with Laney.

"It's true. She's singing a different tune these days. She said she would gladly 'welcome me into the fold.' She even texted me an apology."

"That's my mother, using modern conveniences to do her bidding."

"I don't really blame her for the text. It's not like we're communicating by any other means these days. I think having Ryder freeze her out is about all she can take. Rumor has it, she fired Meg."

"*No.*" My mother worships the ground her mini-me walks on. "Go figure. Maybe that old tiger can change her stripes. Maybe she'll even let Cole into the 'fold.' She made it pretty clear how she feels about him."

"She didn't." Laney looks desperately sad for me.

"She did. She came over and said it was Cole or the Valentine's benefit, and I chose Cole."

Her mouth falls open. "I'm so sorry." Laney knows how much hurt my mother is capable of, and, I know for a fact, neither of us wants to put Cole through my mother's barbed wringer. I guess it'll be me cutting my mother out of my life next.

My phone goes off—it's another mysterious text. "One thousand red velvet cupcakes for the animal shelter fundraiser—by tomorrow night?" It comes out perplexed far more than it ever does excited. It's becoming clear I'm losing my enthusiasm for these back-to-back neck-breaking orders. "Wow, I must have really hit the big time. You really think my mom is behind this?"

"Maybe." She stares at my phone in disbelief. "One thousand red velvet cupcakes. *Ooh* save a couple for me, would you?"

"Will do." I make a face. "Something isn't sitting well with me."

"Are they paying you?"

"In cash on delivery each and every time." My bank account isn't complaining. I tried to pay Cole back for springing for all those supplies he helped me with in the beginning, but he wouldn't hear of it. Poor Cole. I'm almost afraid to tell him about this. "I'd better get going."

Laney and I say our goodbyes, and I bump into my handsome brother on my way out the door.

"Your other half is ready and waiting." I mock sock him on my way out into the cold to brave the elements.

"Stay for a couple minutes. I want to catch up. Maybe we can get dinner somewhere, and you can tell me everything my sweet little sis has been up to." He gives a little wink.

"Can't. I've got another ginormous order to fill in a ridiculous amount of time. I'll be lucky if I'm not kicked out of school by the end of the week."

"What are you talking about?"

"I may have missed a class or two."

"*Roxy*." He closes his eyes a moment. "Tell them you can't fill the order."

"No way. If word gets out that I'm a quitter, I'll never live to bake in this town again."

"Shit." He cuts a quick glance over to Laney. "All right, but don't worry about it too much. I'm betting you won't be getting these 'ginormous' orders anymore."

"That might not be such a bad thing—although I can't really complain. It *is* what I wanted. Anyway, have a great time tonight." I give him a quick hug.

"You, too. Save a few of those cupcakes for me. Red velvet's my favorite."

"Will do."

I get all the way up to the apartment and bake my ass off by myself. If there's one thing I'm up for it's a challenge.

I'm halfway through with my baking spree when it hits me.

I never told Ryder I was baking red velvet.

❧✦☙

I wait until my last batch is done before heading over to the Black Bear. I texted Laney some ridiculous question just to see where my not-so-sweet brother may be. The music is pumping, and the bodies are jumping, all a sure sign Cole will be stuck here for the next few hours. I should be happy that the Edwards' bar is doing so well on their own since I seriously doubt my brother furnished them with patrons like he did me.

"Hey!" Baya jumps up and gives me a hug. "Whoa, no offense, you look like hell, girl."

"None taken. I just spent the last eight hours baking another thousand cupcakes."

"No freaking way!" Her eyes bug out in horror.

"*Yes* freaking way." Somehow all of the deception involved in my brother's scheme demands an explanation. "Have you seen Ryder around anywhere?"

"He's in the back, playing pool."

"Perfect."

She takes off to tend to her tables, and I spot Cole behind the bar, and my heart melts a little. The light hits him just right, and he looks like a god illuminated from the inside. I'm so lucky to have someone like Cole in my life. I can't believe he was right here at Whitney Briggs under my nose this entire time.

I take a step in his direction and notice a familiar blonde seated in front of him, talking a mile a minute as he mixes her a drink—Melanie Harrison.

I speed over just as the girl next to her leans over, and I not-so-accidentally take up her seat.

"Hey, beautiful." Cole swoops over.

"Pink Panty Dropper, please—virgin." I sink a little in my seat. I have no plans on enlisting anybody to hold my hair tonight. In fact, the only person I want holding me later is Cole.

"Funny"—Melanie looks up at me from under her forest of fake lashes—"he just called me the same thing. *Beautiful*." She winks up at Cole, but I doubt he heard.

My stomach turns at the thought. I doubt he called her anything, so I choose to ignore her adolescent attempt to get under my skin.

"Why don't you go dip yourself in a vat of buttercream and run into the nearest fraternity, maybe then you'll get some genuine attention."

The music switches up to some obnoxious pop song that gnawed on me all last summer, and then it hits me, its performed by none other than Steal-Your-Man LeAnn. I swear in a perfect world she'd blow a vocal cord, or, better yet, cheat on Aiden and let him know how much abject misery a heartbreak like that is capable of.

Cole slides my glorified pink lemonade over, and I give a sultry smile up at the ebony-haired god. It's all I can do to keep from bowing to him.

"Lucky you"—he drills those angst-riddled eyes into mine—"you got the last cherry." He gives a quick wink.

"I'm not the only one getting lucky tonight," I purr.

"Oh, yeah?" He leans in. His chin tucked low, his lids hooded over with lust. "Who else is getting lucky tonight?" His eyes widen a notch with boyish anticipation.

"*You.*" I hold back the smile dying to break loose on my face.

A group of guys flag him down, and he blows me a kiss before heading to the other end of the bar.

I hop off my seat, and Melanie snatches at my arm. "Bedding Brighton tonight, are we?" She averts her eyes as if it were cliché in some way. "You want any tips?" Melanie leans in, her cleavage crusading for my attention.

"No. You can keep both your culinary and coital tips to yourself. I've got this."

"Of course, you've got this. You've probably slept with him a million times."

"What's that supposed to mean?" I'm not the one in a sorority known for its sexual shenanigans. She's in Alpha Chi, my cousin Aubree's, ex-sorority. Not that my cousin is a testament to the sorority's greatness, more like a testament to its budding psychosis. Aubree is set to go on trial for attempting to murder Baya by way of drugging her and shoving her off a bridge last fall. I shake all thoughts of my psychotic family out of my head for now.

"Of course, you're knocking boots—*combat* boots." She glances down and makes a face at my footwear. "Anyway, you're living with him so it's to be expected." She rolls her eyes. "Look, everyone sleeps with Cole. It's a right of passage. I get it. It's not like I'm calling you a skank. Relax. I was just going to fill you in on some of his favorite positions."

My insides explode in a hot ball of acid, and the very real threat of reprising my vomit routine pulsates through me.

I glance over at him at the far end of the bar as he entertains a group of coeds while gyrating his cocktail shaker over his chest.

"Did you sleep with Cole?" I ask, but I have a feeling I know the answer. He probably slept with all those girls at the end of the bar as well.

"*Yes*." She says it slow as if I were severely feeble-minded for having to ask. "Have *you* slept with Cole?" She shakes her head as if she were asking a rhetorical question.

My mouth falls open, and not a sound comes out.

"Oh, my gosh! You're a Cole Brighton virgin!" She gives a little whoop before covering her mouth. "I swear I didn't think you people existed. You're like a fabled creature around these parts."

"Shut up, Mel." If anyone can drive me right back to the brink of hating society, it's Melanie Harrison. I don't waste a second heading for the pool room in the back. Melanie shouts something about the competition— something about swapping recipes, or maybe it was positions. Crap. Just the thought of Cole loving her like that makes my skin crawl.

Ryder nods at me as I speed in his direction.

Laney is busing a table nearby, and Bryson is standing next to my brother with a pool stick in hand.

"What's up little sis?" He reverts his attention to the balls breaking on the table.

"Hey, Ryder—or should I call you Mr. Banana-Chocolate-Lemon-Raspberry-Red-Velvet?" His face bleaches out. "So you *are* the one behind these manic orders I've been getting. *Why?*" I bark it in his face because I think I know.

"Ryder!" Laney smacks him over the arm.

Ryder closes his eyes as Laney butts her shoulder into mine awaiting his answer.

"Because"—he gives that look that says *I'm sorry* long before his lips do—"I thought maybe if I kept you busy, it would buy some time for you to see what an idiot that guy you're living with is."

And there it is.

There are so many things I could say to him like *you're just like Mom*, or *thanks for the cash I'll be laughing all the way to the bank right after I roll out of bed with my new boyfriend,* but I don't.

Instead I haul back and deck him right in the jaw.

Ryder stumbles back onto the table.

Bank shot.

Cole

Laney runs out and yells something about Roxy, so I hop over the bar and follow her to the back. There's a brawl breaking out with Ryder and... Roxy?

I help Bryson pluck her off her brother, kicking and screaming, but if I had it my way, I would have let her kick the crap out of him just a little longer.

"Holy shit." I try not to laugh while wrapping my arms around her tight. "Are you okay?"

"Yes." She buries her face in my chest a moment. "I mean no. Do you think you can take me home?"

Bryson nods over to me. "Go ahead, man, I'll close out your shift." He shakes his head at Rox. "Save the sibling rivalry for the holidays. I don't want to have to kick you out of the bar."

"Sorry." She digs her fingers into my back as she says it, and my dick perks up like a reflex.

"What happened?" I'm not moving until I find out what this idiot did to drive Roxy to the point of no return.

"You want to know what happened?" She shoots her brother a look that could slice his balls off. "He's been running us ragged so we wouldn't *do* each other." She leans into him, and he winces as if she were going to clock him again. "But don't worry about that ginormous order you put in today. I'll be sure to get the cupcakes to the animal shelter on time. Too bad for you, though, because my fee just doubled. Now if you don't mind, I'm going home to *fuck* my boyfriend."

Ryder winces as if he were just bitch-slapped. And in a way he was.

Roxy takes me by the hand and leads me out of the bar.

A sly smile creeps up my lips. I've never been with a girl as ballsy as Roxy before.

Who the hell am I kidding? That smile is on my face because I'm about to get laid. And with Roxy it really will feel like the very first time.

I drive us home, and she's pretty quiet all the way over.

We take the elevator up without saying a single word, and with each step toward the apartment, it's starting to feel a little less probable that my dick will be getting the attention it craves.

Damn. I guess it wasn't meant to be tonight. But Rox is pretty upset. I get that.

The apartment is lit up with the scent of chocolate. I take in a deep lungful and feel that familiar carbohydrate high hit me as if it were opium. Cupcakes are laid out over the counter for what looks like miles.

"You want me to help frost some of those?" I offer.

"We can make the frosting, but it's cream cheese—it needs to be refrigerated until delivery day."

The table and counters are all lined with stacks and stacks of pink boxes. "You did all this by yourself?"

"Yeah, you got a problem with that?" She huffs it out, and, for a second, I think she's joking.

"Yeah, I got a problem with that." I pull her in by the hips and chase her eyes with mine until she looks up at me. "What's wrong? Talk to me."

"Everything's wrong." She pushes my hands off her waist and pulls out a mixing bowl. She dumps in cup after cup of confectioners sugar until there's a plume of dust mushrooming out of it like a nuclear bomb just exploded.

"Let me help. We're a team remember?" I step in behind her and land a kiss on the back of her neck.

"Are we a team?" She jerks away. "Or, at the end of the day, am I just going to be another *member* of the team?"

Where the hell is this coming from? "Did something happen that I should know about?"

"I talked to Melanie tonight at the bar." Roxy yanks the drawers open and closed until she finds the utensils she's looking for.

I think I know where this is going.

"You know what she asked?" Her eyes expand with fire in them. "If I was up on all your favorite positions because apparently she *is*."

"I never said I was an angel."

"No, you just sleep with girls with that name. Look, I get it, you've been around."

"And I didn't hide it."

"I never said you did." She screams it out so loud, the windows rattle.

"Then why do I feel like I'm being punished for something?" I shout back.

"Don't you yell at me!" She grabs a fistful of confectioners sugar and pelts it at my chest. The room explodes in a cloud.

A low-riding smile plays on my lips. "Did you just powder bomb me, Capwell?"

She narrows her gaze. Her features soften a notch, and I can tell she's vacillating on how far she's willing to ride her anger tonight. Her brother may have lit the flame, but it's me who's getting burned in the deal.

I reach over and grab a handful of the soft sugar and hold it in the air.

Roxy takes a quick breath. "Don't even think about it."

I gently land my hand over the top of her hair and grind in the fine powder until it looks as if she's wearing a white wig.

"Damn, you're going to look hot when you're eighty." My lips twitch, but I keep a straight face. If she's committed to this argument, I may as well fake like I am, too.

Roxy huffs a dull laugh before picking up a measuring cup filled with fudge, and I take a step back.

"Here, let me help you." I pull off my T-shirt nice and slow. "I'm sure you're going to want to lick it off. Right?"

"Ha!" She barks while baptizing my body with the warm syrup.

I pick up a piping bag filled with raspberry jelly off the counter and drizzle it into her cleavage.

"How does it feel?"

Roxy grabs a fistful of sugar and plucks my jeans open before powdering my balls. "Just as good as that."

Her eyes settle on mine still locked in a rage, and I'd be lying myself into hell if I didn't say I was secretly enjoying the shit out her little temper tantrum.

"How about we wash each other down"—I land my lips an inch from hers—"with our tongues."

Her eyes reduce to slits. That I'd-like-to-punch-you-in-the-throat look crosses her face.

"I bet you say that to all the girls."

"I'm saying it to you."

Roxy slaps me over the chest. "And what about next week, or next month, or even next year?"

"You, you, and *you*." I land a rough kiss over her lips before pulling away. "I only want you, cupcake" I whisper. "Now and forever."

She bites down on her lower lip, her eyes filling with water.

"Shut up and fuck me." Roxy jumps up on my hips, crashing her lips to mine, and I stumble back into the table sending a stack of pots to the floor in a clatter.

Tonight, I'm all about following orders.

Roxy turns up the heat on those wild kisses, and, for the first time ever, it feels as if I'm under a lingual assault. I hold her up by the thighs and lean her against the wall, bearing my mouth down on hers until our kisses feel like a punishment. I slip my fingers up her sweater and unhook her bra—reach around and land my hands over her tits and groan. Shit. My stomach wrenches, and I'm right there ready to lose it. I don't remember second base ever getting me off so fast.

"So?" She backs up, her mascara slightly smudged. She looks gorgeous beyond words. "What's your favorite position, Brighton?" It streams from her with an angry edge, and I'm not going to deny liking it.

I unbutton her jeans and peel them off. I pluck off her sweater and bra all in one fell swoop. My eyes travel up and down her body as she stands here in nothing but her pretty pink underwear, and that smile I've been fighting breaks through just enough.

"This is my favorite position, cupcake," I say, hitching my thumbs in her panties and watching them sail to the floor. "Right here with you." I meet her gaze, and she softens just enough.

I pick her right back up and land her against the wall, working fast and furious to pluck the condom out of my wallet and roll it on without our lips ever leaving one another. I suppose this isn't the best time to show off that I can manage the task with my eyes closed. God knows I'm ready and willing to impress her with a hell of a lot more if she'll let me, and it looks as if she's about to do just that.

Her kisses increase with fury. Roxy pours all her pent up rage into me as she tugs at my hair, rakes her nails over my back.

My hand rides up from her thigh, and my fingers touch down in her heated slick, soft as velvet.

A groan gets buried in her throat as she grinds her hips into my chest begging for more.

My dick throbs rock hard and ticked that it hasn't been invited to the party yet, so I go for it. I gently push in and watch Roxy's head knock into the wall, her eyes roll into her skull as she lets out a cry that says everything I've waited to hear.

I pull her in by the back of the neck and cover her mouth with mine. Roxy sinks over my dick with her body, her fingers digging into my shoulders all the way down.

I take her against the wall like that, pressing in deep until it feels as if I'm about to burst with just one thrust. Her mouth melts over mine as I jolt her into the wall over and over. Roxy heaves as I squeeze my hands into her hips and move her over me with a burst of energy that's just this side of barbaric. I've never had a girl in the kitchen—against the wall—never had it so damn primal and necessary.

A picture hanging above us rattles in tune with my thrusts, the entire apartment sounds as if it's about to collapse with its deafening clap.

It feels as if my world is about to detonate, in every good way.

9

Nothing Tastes Better
Than Sex Cake

Roxy

When I was younger, my friends would talk about what it would be like to "go to bed with a guy," and I would cringe. I imagined myself with my hair in rollers, a green facial mask on, and the most unflattering flannel pajama dress known to man—white with yellow printed daisies just like my mother used to make me wear. How could a cute boy ever want to see me like that, I would wonder. But, now that I'm older, I see that even with my hair covered in powdered sugar, my naked body coated with raspberry jam as if a baking massacre just occurred—Cole still very much wants to see me like this. He holds that lustful look on his face, and I know now that I've had nothing to worry about all along.

My eyes slit open, and I watch as Cole thrusts his head back, his lids shut tight, his brows narrow in as if he were in pain. He's pumping his body into mine, harder and faster, digging his fingers into my hips, squeezing as if he's about to pinch right through. He's so lost in his delirium. It catapults me into the stratosphere knowing that I'm responsible for that. That I'm the one who put that lusty look on his face—it's my body making him convulse with pleasure. I own this man in the very best way.

He bucks forward burying his lips in my neck and jolts. "I'm coming," he hisses as he trembles over me with his release.

The picture stops quaking. The chair stops slamming up against the wall from the tension we've put on this small corner of the kitchen. The room clots up with a bionic silence that makes my ears pulsate in turn—leaving nothing but the sound of our panting.

His even heated breaths cool over my chest.

"Shit." He huffs with the hint of a laugh. "I wasn't expecting that."

"I plan on keeping you on your toes."

He pulls back and beams that million-dollar smile. His teeth go on and off like a flashlight until his head falls into me again. Cole rides slow, easy kisses up my neck all the way to my lips.

"Sorry," he moans over my lips.

"For the STDs?" A part of me cringes because I pray it's not true.

"I'm clean, I swear." He pulls back and gives a wry smile.

"Oh, yeah? And how do you know? Did that magic eight ball on the coffee table tell you?"

"Because"—he lands a wet kiss over my lips—"I just had all my shots at the vet, cupcake. That's how I know." He pulls out and cinches his jeans up a notch. "Shower or bed?"

"There's no way you're dragging me to that lice-infested love den of yours." A dark laugh rumbles in my throat. "I hadn't really thought of having sex with you anywhere in this apartment. I'm odd like that."

His brows pitch giving him an ironically innocent look, and a dull ache explodes in my gut because I can't believe this beautiful boy was inside me, rough and greedy, taking me like a beast in heat.

"Not in the apartment, huh?" Cole seems genuinely perplexed by my lack of coital creativity. "You know what I like better than imagining where we'll have sex?" His affect flattens, his lids hood low, and he looks sexy as all hell. "Showing you."

Cole pulls my arms up high and lunges into me with a kiss that spells *I love you* with every cell in his body. His hot mouth moves lower as he gently pulls me toward the hall. I know where this is going. He's already hinted at it, and I'm almost looking forward to it since the sticky raspberry goo he marked me with has dripped down to my toes.

"How come I'm naked, and you still have half your clothes on?" I bite down over his ear until he gives a hard groan.

"Because I'm a dirty bastard." His lids stay low. His chest pumps hard as if he just ran a marathon.

"Knew it." My fingers glide down his chest, straight to that stream of barely there hair that leads to penis places where dirty condoms live. I stop shy of the sticky mess and kiss him instead.

"I'm right there with you." Cole flicks off his shoes, and they shoot across the room like missiles. His jeans drop in the hall, and he steps right out of them. He whisks us into the bathroom and turns on the shower. I switch on the light, shocked at my own bravery. Here I am standing under the surprise of illumination—naked with the exception of my hair falling over my chest. If I turn around, he'll see that I should probably utilize that workout garb I wear every day, and that my sweatshirts are mostly for show because I don't spend any of my free time doing Pilates or yoga. The truth is I eat cupcakes like they were nutritional supplements and down eight cups of coffee just to keep my fluids up. If I ever need a blood transfusion, they'd better hook me up to a latte drip, or I'll be a gonner as soon as the caffeine wears off.

"And what about these?" I tug at his boxers.

Cole moves with the dexterity of a magician and discards the condom and his boxers. He pulls me into the almost scalding shower way too fast for me to ever properly check him out.

"Things are about to get hotter." Cole stands in front of me as if we're about to dance. The water sprays over my back, drumming soft as tears before trickling down my legs. A silver plume of steam envelops us. His eyes are glued to mine as he digs his fingers into the back of my hair. "You know what I thought that first day in the bar?"

"That you'd land me in bed a lot sooner than this?"

His chest bucks. "Technically, I still haven't landed you in bed."

"You will." I touch my finger under his chin and pull him forward as if he were on a string. "And if you're very, very lucky, I'll let you repeat the effort."

His lips curve up on one side. That cocky smirk that drives me fucking insane takes over, and I want nothing more than to jump his bones. And, since I'm short on girly sentiments, I hop up on his hips and wrap my legs around his slippery waist. Cole rushes in with a kiss, wild as a hurricane—an entire wash of emotions releasing in my mouth. His bare skin against mine feels like the most erotic thing in the world—hard and hot, chiseled in all the right places. It's Christmas, and my birthday, and every good thing I've ever felt in my life, exploding over my senses all at once.

"God, I love you," I pant into his ear. I don't bother telling him I've not once said those words to Aiden. They were words for other people, other ridiculous morons who bought into the fantasy of expensive weddings and cheesy Valentine's Day traditions. Something about Cole has unwound me, unraveled me like a tightknit sweater, and I can breathe and smile, and, for the very first time, I can see the glimmer of an expensive wedding on the horizon. Not to mention I plan on making our first Valentine's Day as cheesy as possible with rose petals on the mattress and enough hot fudge to bathe us both in.

"I love you, cupcake," he says it serious right into my ear, and I suck in a breath with the erotic rush it gave me. I soak the words in—drink them down right through to my porous bones. Holy hell, he loves me.

Cole melts kisses down my neck, down my chest before dropping to his knees. His mouth lands hot over my belly button and dips in and out as I give a mean shudder.

My palm flattens against the cool tile. My breathing grows erratic as Cole dips lower until his searing mouth finds a home over the most tender part of me. He pushes my thighs apart with his strong, thick fingers as my hands dig into his hair.

His tongue rides over me soft at first then at a quickened pace. The universe expands and retracts around me. Every molecule in my body stands at attention as he explodes over me with a fit of passion. The room quakes. My body seizes and writhes while the pressure builds thick and urgent as the essence of who I am begs to rip from my skin. This thing with Cole—*love*—is something foreign to me, far too outrageously delicious to have ever happened before.

His tongue runs wild over me, and the pace of the world picks up. Pulses of electricity zip along my nerves setting my skin on fire. My past evaporates like a vapor, and this very moment reassigns itself as a rebirth, the genesis of the rest of my days.

A cry rips from my lungs as my body erupts in a wave of convulsive shivers.

I push him off and hold my hands there, knotted up in his hair, with Cole on his knees for me, and I memorize the moment.

It could be like this always if I wanted.

If I could just keep from screwing things up.

Somehow I doubt this.

⁝⁞

We spend all night tangled up in one another's exhausted arms right there on the living room floor with my comforter thrown over us haphazardly. In the morning my lids flutter as I try to adjust to the harsh light coming in through the window.

I grind to life, and the first thing I see are Cole's perfect lips. God, this boy is beautiful. His dark hair, black as midnight, his long lashes curl perfectly upward. And even in his sleep, he wears that sexy smirk that says, *yeah, you're coming to bed with me.* I was never the jealous type. I couldn't care less about who or what other girls are looking at, but just knowing that Cole gets those bedroom eyes right back makes my stomach pinch with grief. For once, I'd love to be the center of someone's world. I'd love to steal the spotlight in someone's life for more than five minutes before being discarded or cheated on.

I press a quick kiss to his neck, his hard-on already rousing to greet me. My chest rumbles with a laugh as I carefully extract myself from his warm embrace. I toss on his T-shirt and hit the kitchen, pulling out weapons of culinary destruction as quietly as possible.

For as long as I can remember, I have tried to commemorate a special occasion by creating a new confection that I thought somehow captured the magic.

I pull out the ingredients, and as I reach for the eggs, it hits me like a thousand butter soft cupcakes, and I know just what to do to make these extra special.

The thick scent of sugar marrying with butter lights up the room as I bake up a quick batch. There's a hint of cocoa in the air that leaves me swooning to the aroma of my own creation.

A pair of arms slip around me from behind. "Morning."

I glance up as Cole presses a kiss over the top of my head.

"Morning, yourself."

He lets out a hearty groan, and his eyes roll back into his head. "You're killing me with that smell." He walks over to the oven and peeks inside.

"Relax, they're ready." I pull them out and let them cool on the counter. "You know what else is ready?" I wrap my arms around his neck, pulling him in.

He's wearing nothing but a pair of boxers and a grin, and I'm pretty sure that's all that Cole Brighton should ever wear.

"Me for you?" He plants a kiss just shy of my ear, and my toes curl from that one simple act.

"I was going to say *me* for *you,* but I think I like it the other way around even better."

Cole sobers up. His expression softens as he pours his affection straight into my eyes. "You're really special to me, Rox." His lips twitch like he might lose it. "Do you want this with me?"

A spear of adrenaline shoots through my chest like a rocket. "Yes—hell, yes, I want this with you. You're the best surprise life has ever given me." My insides pulsate as if they were somehow trying to make an escape because, deep down, I'm afraid I've pushed him away with how desperate I sound.

His dimples dig in deep. His brows lengthen like birds in flight, and my heart soars with relief.

"I'm glad." He ticks his head back toward the table at the stacks and stacks of bakery boxes filled with cupcakes. "What time do these need to be delivered?"

"About three-thirty."

"Good." He glances at the clock on the microwave. "I want to help you finish them and make sure they get there on time. Even if your brother is responsible, I'm sure whoever's expecting them is looking forward to having one of the best cupcakes in the world."

"Thank you." I dot his lips with a kiss, and for the first time in my life, I feel normal—not like some freak or ball of anger, just simply like me. "Speaking of the best cupcake in the world. I made these special just for you." I hand him a warm cupcake fresh from the tin.

"Chocolate's my favorite." He takes a bite and freezes. His apple-green eyes lay over mine, and he doesn't move. Cole doesn't breathe. He finishes it off in a few quick bites, and a roar gurgles from his throat.

"I like to call it nothing's-better-than-sex-with-Cole-Brighton cake. I bet I could sell them by the dozen just standing outside sorority row." There's a fun fact.

He shakes his head. His eyes hold a smile just for me. "How about we keep this one just for us."

"Oh, yeah?" I run my finger along his strong jawline. "Why's that?"

"Because the only person 'Cole Brighton' wants to have sex with now and forever is you." He scoops me into his arms, and I let out a little scream as I fall back into his strong embrace. "We've got a few hours. Why don't I give you a demonstration?"

"By all means, show me what you've got."

"I plan to."

He lands us on the couch with his mouth hot over mine, his hands exploring my body with a heated restraint.

Having sex with Cole both now and forever?

I can get used to that.

But a warning goes off deep inside me that says *don't count on it*.

Cole

The sun never bothered to show today, just one long, slate grey sky as a storm front pushes on the horizon.

Roxy and I unload a thousand cupcakes from the back of my truck and drop them off at the animal shelter where kids and parents alike wait to dig into the delectable desserts and hopefully adopt a dog or two.

Roxy gets back in the truck and just as I'm about to do the same, her cruising-for-a-bruising brother pops up.

I nod over at him because I'm pretty damn sure whatever might fly out of my mouth won't be half as nice.

"What the hell are you doing with my sister, man?" He says it quiet like he genuinely wants to know. "We both know what kind of guy you are."

"What kind of guy is that?" I grit it out with my adrenaline pumping because I think I know where this conversation is headed.

"The kind who doesn't know how to keep it in his pants—Whitney Briggs' very own white trash."

"Fuck you." I butt my shoulder into his as I make my way to the truck and take off without ever looking back.

Damn douche is lucky I didn't run him over for the hell of it.

"What's got you going?" Roxy leans into the side mirror and makes a face. "Never mind. Would you please ignore him? I swear he thinks he's protecting me. I'll have to remind him I don't need protecting anymore."

My stomach cinches. "Funny you should say that." Actually, it's not funny. Just the thought of what went on last semester makes the acid rise to the back of my throat. "I sort of did the same to Baya when she started dating Bryson."

Roxy reaches over and rests her hand on my thigh.

"I know," she whispers. "That's why I'm hoping you'll cut him some slack." She straightens in her seat. "Hey...since you're an expert on being an obnoxious big brother, why don't you talk to him? You know, really get down to bare bones and let him know you get it. That you were there once yourself."

"I'll try, but I'm pretty sure he's got some preconceived ideas about me that are going to be hard to turn away from." Like the fact he thinks I'm white trash. And, in truth, nothing could have pissed me off faster. I'm not really in the mood to hug it out with him just yet.

"I hope we can get over it. I can't stand the thought of there being a rift between Ryder and me. It's like my entire family has blown apart. Not that we were perfect or anything, but it was all we had—all we knew, and I'd give anything to have that back."

My heart breaks for her because I know exactly what it's like to have your family blown apart. The Capwell's are lucky because, for one, they're all still in the land of the living. My family is never going to be put back together again, at least not on this planet.

"I'm going to do everything I can to make things right with your brother, Rox." I reach over and squeeze her knee. "I promise you that."

"Thank you. I can't tell you how much that means to me."

It's going to be harder than shit, but I'd do anything for Rox. I pull off the highway and head east until we hit Golden Cove.

"Oh my, God, it's beautiful." Roxy pulls me in by the arm as we gaze out at the frozen shoreline. A thin layer of frost covers the sand as far as the eye can see. The Atlantic is a murky grey with deep navy veins just beneath the surface. The water spreads wide and vast, black in its deepest part. It's days like this the ocean looks as if it has a soul.

"Love it," I say as I drive the truck right off the concrete and onto the sand. I drive down to the waterline and park with the rear facing the ocean.

"How about we crawl into the back and watch the show?"

Her lips twitch side to side as she pinches a wry smile. "I thought we *were* the show."

"I like where you're going." We head to the back, and I leave the tailgate open along with the rear window. I had the bed carpeted when they planted the shell on the back, and, right about now, I'm pretty damn glad.

I lay out a couple of old sleeping bags, and we crawl in.

Her lids lower, her mouth falls open as she washes her gaze over me. "Ten bucks says I can take my clothes off first."

"Go." I take off my shirt and simply watch the show as she busies herself by peeling off her yoga pants, that long sweatshirt that keeps falling off her shoulder.

"Hey, you cheated!" She mock punches me in the stomach.

"Whoa." I catch her tiny fist and trap it in my hands. "It's not cheating if I'm still dressed. Besides, I'd be an idiot not to watch you strip. You do it quite nicely by the way. Have you considered it as a professional career?"

"Shut up, and kiss me."

"Yes, ma'am." I lean in and land my mouth over hers. Roxy's lips are two swollen pillows I'd love to spend the night on. "You're in your bra and panties." I point out. "This race looks like it's still wide open to me." I do my best to wrangle off my jeans and boxers, tossing my shoes and socks in the corner. "I win."

"Yeah?" Rox crawls over on all fours like a vixen, and my dick springs to life unapologetically. "Maybe I *let* you win." She runs her tongue up my neck, and I let out an involuntary groan. "Maybe I wanted to *watch*?"

"Nice." My hands glide down her back and round out her lace-covered bottom. I run my fingers in the seam of her panties, dipping down low until I feel how wet and ready she is. My finger dips in and out nice and slow as a choking sound sputters from her throat. This is heaven.

I reach back and snatch a condom out of my pocket. With Roxy in my life I want to be ready and willing, anytime, anyplace.

"You won't be needing that." She takes it from me and tosses it behind her back. "Not yet anyway." Roxy comes up for a kiss before gliding her way back down my chest, down my abs, never taking her mouth off me.

"Oh shit," I whisper. I'd be lying if I didn't say that one of the first things I imagined her doing to me was just this. Rox pushes my knees apart and bows her head into me with her ass sticking straight up in the air, and just beyond that there's nothing but the deep blue sea. Best damn view ever.

Her lips seal over my body, and she rides me long and hard with that mouth of hers until I'm out of my fucking mind. I grab her by the hair and push her in deeper just before I lose it and pluck her off.

"You didn't have to do that," she says out of breath, making her way back up to my lips.

"I did if I want to do this." I seal my mouth over hers and show her how thankful I am she just treated me to one hell of a spectacular view—that she just made one of my chief fantasies come true.

Roxy is a fantasy come true.

And I'm looking forward to living out this fantasy for the rest of my life if she'll have me.

ଚ୍ଚଠଷ

A week floats by. I've got one serious spring in my step, and I can honestly say Roxy put it there.

"So what's the deal?" Bryson asks as we walk past the field on the way to our final class of the day. It's hard to believe we'll be graduating in just a few short months.

"She's graciously let me sleep in her bed. But don't yap it to her brother. I'd hate to see his balls catch fire when he finds out. On second thought, if burning balls are involved..."

"Trust me, Ryder won't hear it from me." He holds back a laugh. "Besides, I thought something like this might happen. That's why Baya and I took the room farthest from your apartment—no adjoining walls."

I shoot him a look. "Don't you ever reference the fact you sleep in the same bed with my sister—got that?" I'm only half-kidding. My lunch just did a flip in my stomach.

"You're coming in loud and clear, *Ryder*."

"Yeah, I forgot to laugh."

"I bet at the end of the day, you and Ryder will be good friends. He's a nice guy once you get to know him. He's Laney's main squeeze, and Rox and Laney are tight. He's one of *my* good friends, so you have to like him. If you don't, you're going to ruin our little hexagon of love."

"Shut up before I sock you in the nuts." A thought comes to me. "You know what, dude? Why don't you try the pep talk with your good pal, Ryder? I'm thinking he's the one you need to get to drink the Kool Aid. I swear, I've got nothing against the guy. I get it—he's her brother. I'm Baya's brother, and half the time I still feel like beating your ass."

"Nice."

"You know what I mean, or at least you will when Annie gets serious with someone."

"Yeah, well, that's not happening. Annie's moving back home with my mom as soon as she graduates from college, and they're going to collect cats until they're old and grey. The end."

I bark out a laugh. "You wish, dude. There's some guy out there right now just hoping to meet a girl like Annie." Bryson's eyes bug out. "Granted, he'll get his ass handed to him by you and Holt, but, eventually, it'll happen." I slap him five before we part ways. "Don't you worry your pretty little head too much. I'm sure the odds of you finding her on her knees in front of his naked ass are slim to none."

That's exactly how I found him and Baya last fall—still wish I could gouge the memory out of my mind.

"I'm going to kill you."

"Catch you later," I say, jogging toward Kristoff Hall where my last class of the day is. I run up the steps and into the dark building and smack into—

"Angel." Crap. In fact, I would have preferred stepping in a big steaming pile of greasy shit than be face-to-face with this girl.

"Hi Cole." Her entire face reconfigures into a look of exaltation. "I've missed you. Have you missed me?" An ear-to-ear grin plasters onto her face, eager for my like-minded answer.

"Actually—" Crap. I don't have the heart to tell her to get lost.

"I baked these for you." She thrusts a small paper bag in my face before I can get a word in. "They're chocolate chips with M&Ms. I thought what better way to your heart than through your stomach."

I pause for a minute because this isn't adding up to some innocent run in. We're standing smack in front of my Business Economics class, and I figure out pretty quick this is very much planned.

"Cookies, huh?" Too bad for her—Roxy beat her to my heart and my stomach. "Look, I don't think I should take these."

"Oh, sure you can!" Her eyes widen the size of tennis balls. "I can make more. My roommate is a master baker—kind of like yours." She nods, completely clueless that Rox and I have a lot more going on than sharing the rent.

"Okay, look, I gotta run. But thanks for these. I'm sure they'll be delicious."

I give a quick pat to her back and bolt into class.

Maybe if I continue to keep her at an arms length, she'll get the message and go away.

Or maybe she won't.

I'm betting on the latter.

10

Brownie Points

Roxy

After my Entrepreneurship and Small Business class fiasco finishes for the day, I collect my things and try to scamper out the door. This is usually the part where Aiden injects his tongue down LeAnn's throat because it's obviously the only way he can get her to stop giggling. I swear she's part hyena—boyfriend-stealing hyena—but deep down I know that's not true. No "real" boyfriend could ever be stolen. A little part of their cold, black heart has to want to leave.

I wonder if Cole has it in him to stay, or if, after the novelty of what we have wears off, he'll simply start bringing home the girls again and racking up more points on that sexual scoreboard of his.

A light tap hits my shoulder. "You mind if we talk for a minute?" An ultra-light girly voice streams from behind—

LeAnn. Suddenly I want to kick in her kneecaps for sounding so annoying.

I glance up at her with a smiling Aiden by her side who looks as if he just ate the canary. A visual of feathers sprouting from LeAnn's ass comes to mind, and I shake it away.

"What?" I pull all the sweetness from my voice as I cinch my backpack over my shoulders. I don't really mind that I come across like a hard ass. In fact, I want to. I want to come across like a bitch with an attitude that no sane person would think of crossing. But, then again, I hardly believe either LeAnn or Aiden qualify as sane.

"Well"—she looks to Aiden and giggles—"I know this might be awkward for you." She squints into me, her mouth puckering as if she were eighty. "I'm having an open-air concert this Friday. And I was thinking"—she drives a finger into her cheek, making her look too stupid to live—"would you mind donating some cupcakes for the event?"

"*Donating*?" I practically choke on the word. Excuse me, I want to say, but I wasn't the one featured in Forbes magazine as profit churner of the year like the pop princess in front of me. No, I would not like to *donate* to your little warbling fest.

"Yeah, you know." She gives a few rapid blinks as if a gnat just flew in her eye. "I'm a judge for the Sticky Quickie baking competition and honey bear says you're going to be competing, so I can't actually pay you for anything or else you would be automatically disqualified."

Gah! She's like a plague on my existence. She's going to single handedly take down my future internship at the Sticky Quickie, and she's too blonde to realize it.

I stop shy of glaring at *honey bear.*

"Anyhoo"—she wraps an arm around Aiden, and I continue to pretend he's invisible, thus demoting him to the relevancy of a dust mite, annoying yet unavoidable—"I've already asked Melanie Harrison, and she'll be baking her signature Ecstasy Delights, and I thought if you had a signature cupcake, you could make up a bunch of those, too. At first I wasn't going to ask because of our shaky history, but honey bear said it would be the right thing to do since both you and Melanie will be representing Whitney Briggs."

Again with the honey bear. I glare over at Aiden for a moment. I'd like to dip him in honey and roll him into a pile of fire ants.

"For the record, we aren't representing the university in the competition. We're actually competing *against* each other." Wait, if she's a judge, I might want to hold off before I segue into the part about where exactly it is I'd like to shove a *bunch* of my signature cupcakes. "Come to think of it, yes, I will bring my signature cupcakes to the event. I'd love to donate my time and effort to the student body of Whitney Briggs." I frown at my lame attempt to try and whitewash the fact I'm kissing the same ass my ex-boyfriend is slobbering over.

I speed past the two of them toward the door.

"Oh wait, *Foxy!*" she shouts. "I need the name of your signature cupcake to give to my PR department."

PR? Crap. Things are getting serious.

"It's Roxy," I reprimand as gently as possible. "And the name of my signature cupcake is"—it takes everything in me not to say, *cock sucking ex-boyfriend*—"It's called, I love Cole Brighton." My lips twitch. "Actually I think I'll call it the I Slept with Cole Brighton."

"Ooh, I like it. That sounds like fun!" She erupts in a giggle fest, and Aiden is quick to elbow her.

"It is fun. It's the best time of my life, and it tastes like paradise."

She takes up his hand while chortling into him, and, for the first time, I feel nothing—not one hint of rage or heartbreak, not one ounce of hurt.

Cole crops up in my mind, and I have the sudden urge to see him and tell him all about this twisted exchange, especially the moniker I've decided to gift my "signature" cupcake.

I start to head out the door, and my arm is yanked back by the elbow.

Aiden shoves his face in mine, and I can see LeAnn already halfway down the hall. "You think this is funny? That it's some game to get back at me by trying to make me jealous with that tool you're hooking up with? I know all about that idiot. Newsflash, he's not that into you, sweetie." He presses out that sarcastic grin I've grown accustomed to over the years, the one he used when he was losing control and needed to pull his balls off the floor with a net. "From what I hear, he's into just about everyone." He leans in. His eyes still squinting out that cocky smile. "Don't go thinking you're special."

My hand explodes over his face in one thunderous slap before I speed out the door.

I am special damn it.

Only Aiden is too stupid to notice.

ೞೞ

I get home, and Cole chips away at me until I tell him what's wrong. I leave out the little detail of Aiden telling me I wasn't special. No need to press down on a bruise.

Cole offers to take me to dinner, and I don't protest.

We drive out of Hollow Brook and toward downtown Jepson, right into a trendy neighborhood that has an entire row of ritzy restaurants that I'm pretty sure a bartender can't afford. Suddenly, I feel bad that Cole is even entertaining the idea.

"We can find a drive-thru," I offer.

"No way. You've had a rough day. Besides, I'd like to reward you for smacking him today. Just the thought of you using me to make him jealous is laughable."

"It totally is." In all honesty, that's how this whole thing started, but what Cole and I share is one hundred percent real—it's special.

Cole pulls into a lavish sushi restaurant that I haven't been to before. The silver framed building is equipped with dark-tinted windows that stretch from floor to ceiling and it reeks of dollar bills long before we make our way inside.

A row of sushi chefs yell as we enter, and we're seated almost immediately which should clue Cole in on the fact this place is going to drain his tip money for the better half of the month.

"Really, I'm not worth it," I whisper. "Let's just leave. We can go to the Black Bear and split some chili fries."

"No, thanks. I've seen what goes into them." He presses a kiss over my cheek. "And, yes, you're worth it."

"Roxy!" A girl's voice calls from across the way.

It's Laney and Ryder! I jump a little. Nothing makes me happier than my BFF and my favorite big bro even if he's trying to act like a wedge between me and the boy I love. Ryder means well.

We speed over, and Laney is quick to give me a tackle hug. "This is perfect. I've had a crap day, and I can't imagine a better way to turn things around than by running into the two of you." I glance over at Cole who looks less than enthused. "But we totally don't want to impose. So enjoy your night." I give a slight wave.

"No way, Capwell." Laney nods over to the waitress. "Two more will be joining us."

"No, really we don't have to," I hear myself say without any real feeling behind it.

"Yes, you do." Ryder points us to the two empty seats that have miraculously appeared, and both Cole and I comply. "We just sat down. It's perfect timing."

"So are you two celebrating something big?" Cole asks as he peruses the menu.

"Nope." Laney takes a sip from her water. "We eat here just about every night."

"We're boring that way." Ryder gives Laney's shoulder a quick squeeze. Laney and Ryder are anything but boring as evidenced by their panache for sushi that starts off at thirty dollars a roll.

Holy crap. I gawk at the menu. For what it's going to cost to feed the two of us, we can buy an entire aquarium full of sea creatures.

It's becoming pretty clear we're not getting out of here without dropping a couple hundred bucks if we want to satisfy our appetites. Suddenly, my appetite has decreased significantly.

The waitress comes by, and I put in my order, which amounts to water and an appetizer.

"We're together." Cole motions to me before he dips back to the menu.

"Oh, we've got this." Laney insists.

"No, it's fine." Cole glances to the waitress. "I'll have a number fifty six and a number forty three."

Ryder breaks out into a shit-eating grin because we both know poor Cole just referenced the price points since the menu items aren't numbered.

"You know what?" Cole looks back up. "Make that two of each."

Crap.

The waitress finishes taking our orders and disappears.

"How about you guys?" Laney leans into us. "You celebrating something big tonight?"

"Just each other," I offer, and I can't help feel like I just lit a very short fuse when it comes to my brother. I know full well there's bad blood between him and my brand new boyfriend.

Cole wraps his arm around me. "I wanted to do something special for Rox since she had a tough day."

"What happened?" Laney rasps her knuckles over the table as if she wants names. She's always the first to stand up for me. I should have listened to her eons ago when she told me to dump Aiden's sorry ass. Laney is always right.

"Guess who's baking cupcakes for LeAnn Giggle-Box's big Whitney Briggs's burp and chirp?"

"Crap." Her features harden. I can always count on Laney to side with me when the shit hits the fan.

"Crap is right. And I'll be essentially competing with Melanie Harrison because she's donating her signature venereal disease delights to the event as well."

"*Ecstasy* Delights?" Ryder's affect brightens for a moment, and I shoot him a look. "What are you baking?"

"My new signature cupcake." I look over to Cole because I haven't exactly gotten around to telling him the stellar name I chose yet. "It's the, I love Cole Brighton."

Cole's eyes widen. His lips crimp a tiny smile before breaking out that thousand-kilowatt grin of his. "You said that?"

"I meant it." Every word. "Then I promptly changed it to the I Slept with Cole Brighton. I figure it appeals a little more to the masses."

Cole cinches a smile.

"Rox," Ryder moans and closes his eyes as if I just ran over a puppy.

"What? I'm sure if I called it the *I Love My Big Bro,* you'd be singing a different tune."

"Yes, I would," he mutters under his breath.

"What the hell's that supposed to mean?" My mood plummets right along with that grin I've been wearing ever since we sat down. Teaches me to smile. There always seems to be a bucket of crap waiting for me at the end of the deliriously happy rainbow.

"It means I have more longevity." Ryder glances up at me from his menu, and that familiar rage percolates inside me. For one, the fact he won't give this conversation his full attention is pissing me off, and, secondly, this entire conversation sucks.

Cole's chest pumps with a silent laugh at the balls my brother has for dismissing him like that. I have a feeling we won't be staying too much longer. And the way my brother's acting, I wouldn't mind stiffing him with the bill— not that it would ever come near to hurting him the way he's hurting me right now.

"Take it back," I say it low, trying not to cause a scene, but a part of me wants to crawl over the table and shake my brother by the pretentious collar peeking out from under his cashmere sweater. "Cole and I are together, and that's not changing."

Ryder ticks his head back an inch. "How do you know it's not changing?"

Cole leans in ready for a fight. "Because I say it's not. Don't bust her balls. What part of shit day don't you understand?"

"Guys, *relax*." Laney holds her hands out over the table as if she were about to conduct a séance. "Nobody's busting anybody's balls. Ryder was just trying to say that you guys haven't been going out very long and for you to declare your love for him as a part of something that should be recognized with your brand—well, it's kind of out there."

"What?" A flood of rage fills me. Suddenly it feels as if I'm right back with the bitterness, right back to detesting the entire human race, save for a few select people, and I think both Laney and Ryder have just wiped themselves off that list.

"I'm not trying to insult you." Laney gets that I'm-only-doing-this-for-your-own-good look in her eye—the same look she used to give me when she said kick Aiden to the curb, preferably by the balls. "This is all new, and maybe you should call your signature cupcake something more representative of who you really are and what kind of public image you want to portray."

"Like? The unlovable loser who can't keep a guy?"

"Nobody said that," Ryder snips.

"You *implied* it!" I snatch up my purse with one hand and Cole with the other. "You know what? I don't need the two of you in my life to remind me of what a failure I am at things. In fact, why don't you both just stay out of it, and that way you won't have to keep yourselves up at night trying to find new ways to tell me how much my relationship sucks."

"*Roxy*." Ryder's voice carries, and everybody within a three-table span turns to look at us.

"Save it!" I bark. "I never once said to either of you that it wouldn't last. In fact, when it *didn't* last, I was your biggest cheerleader to get you two back together. Boy am I ever sorry."

Cole drops a wad of money on the table, and we fly out of there.

Just what the hell do Laney and Ryder see wrong with my relationship that I don't?

Cole

Who the fuck are Laney and Ryder to cast the first stone?

I pull Roxy in and wrap my arms around her as soon as we get outside the financial fleecing trying to pass off as a sushi bar.

"I'm not walking away from us." I pour each word into her eyes.

Roxy takes a breath and relaxes into me.

"Get me the hell away from here."

"You don't need to ask twice." We get in the truck, and I hit the road. I'd take her home, but I'd love to cleanse our palates first, get both her psycho friend and her mentally-challenged brother off our minds. No thanks to the two of them, Roxy's day has gone from shit to worse. There's no way I'm letting her end her night this way.

"You still okay with a drive-thru?" At this point it's questionable I can even afford that. I dumped all my tip money back there, but there was no way I was going to let Ryder have the satisfaction of bitching about how I walked out on my bill.

"Drive-thru's fine," she growls. "I think it's a public safety issue at this point. I'm ready to claw out the eyes of the next person who looks at me crooked."

My lips twitch, but I hold back the smile. I happen to think Roxy is sexy as all hell when she's fired up.

We hit the nearest burger joint, then drive past Whitney Briggs, up further into the mountains until we pass the river, the hot springs, and a rickety old bridge. I take the road up about as far as it goes and head toward the overlook.

The stars spray out like a million grains of salt—while the city lights of Hollow Brook sparkle back at us like beacons. In the distance, you can see Jepson.

I help Rox into the back of the truck, and we snuggle over the sleeping bags while wolfing down our ninety-nine cent burgers, our shared large fries, and diet Coke.

Roxy's skin holds the scent of vanilla and a dusting of powdered sugar. I bet she tastes like it, too. I take a playful bite out of her neck to confirm my theory, and I'm right.

"This is quickly becoming my favorite place to eat." She rubs her shoulder into mine.

"Just eat?"

"You're my favorite dessert." She pitches her brows before her features fall again. "I'm sorry about everything that happened back there. I'm pretty embarrassed."

"Don't be. I'm sure they were only looking out for you. Give it some time. Once they see me hanging around for ten—twenty years, they'll get the hint I'm not going anywhere."

Her lips twitch with a quiet smile. "This is beautiful." She looks up at the sky as if she were changing the subject.

"I think you're beautiful." I run my fingers over her cheek. Roxy is a sculpture's dream with those high cut cheekbones, those perfect full lips.

"You don't have to compliment me." She looks into my eyes, sad, despondent as if she had given up on some level. "You're going to get lucky either way." A tiny smile breaks free.

"I like the sound of that, but I wasn't buttering you up to get lucky. I mean it. You're the most gorgeous human I've ever laid eyes on. I have to pinch myself at least twice a day to believe a girl like you would have anything to do with someone like me."

"Please, you can have any girl you want, and, believe me, there are enough tally marks on that wall back home to prove it."

"You know what got my attention that day we first met at the Black Bear?" I hitch a shard of hair behind her ear.

"The fact I was more interested in the BTUs your oven could put out than I was in any of your mattress moves?"

"Exactly. You were the one I couldn't have." I shake my head. "And you were the one I wanted from hello."

"Really?" She tucks her thumbnail between her teeth and laughs.

"Yes, really. I took one look in your direction and my entire body demanded to have you. You're hot, and, underneath that tough exterior, sweet as hell. You're perfect, Rox."

"It's cupcake to you." She lies down and nestles her head into the sleeping bag. "I secretly like it when you call me that." Her eyes slit to mine. "Don't tell anyone, or I'll cut you."

"Physical threats, huh? That's one of my favorite things about you. You're not afraid to say how you really feel."

"Cole?" She wraps her arms around me, and I land on my elbows staring down at the most beautiful girl on the planet. "What did you see in all those other skanks you were with?" Her eyes catch the moonlight and glow like copper.

"Not going there." I land a soft kiss over her lips. "They meant nothing. I swear it. I've never felt so fucking gone, so heart stopping in love with anyone in my life."

"So that spell I cast over the first batch of cupcakes I fed you really worked, huh?"

"Enchanted cupcakes?" I tweak my brows, amused at the idea.

"Works every time."

"Newsflash, it didn't work." I land a wet kiss just shy of her ear and blow gently over it until she shudders beneath me. "I didn't need a spell to make me want you.

What I'm feeling is one hundred percent born from my heart. And thank you because I didn't think it existed before I met you."

"Again, no need to score brownie points because you're pretty much guaranteed to dip your wick."

"My wick?" I pull back and examine her. She's funny, and smart, and hot as hell, and Roxy still can't wrap her head around the fact I want her just for who she is.

"So answer my question, what was with the line outside your door?"

"Drop the inquisition." My lips land over hers, and she turns her head.

"It's just that I noticed something, and I wanted to see if you noticed it, too."

Crap. She's really going to ride this horse to the finish line, so I might as well play along.

"The girls." I close my eyes a moment straining every cell in my body trying to figure out some commonality they may have had. "I don't know—they were easy."

"They were all blonde and perky, cheerleader types."

"I'm pretty sure they weren't all blonde." Although, now that I think about it—there might have been a disproportionate amount. "And, if they were, I blame it on the peroxide industry. I bet you good money they were all secretly brunettes." I nuzzle a kiss into her neck, and she giggles. Something in my heart soars just hearing her happy, and knowing I'm the one that made her feel that way makes me feel pretty damn good.

"I guess what I'm getting at is that I'm not really your type, so it made me wonder—"

"*Whoa.*" I land a finger over her nose. "Hold it right there." I trace her lips out before dipping the tip of my finger into her mouth. "I don't have a *type.*" My gaze softens. "I have a girlfriend." I entwine our fingers. "And I love her so damn much, I feel like I might explode." A grin presses out of me, and I can't help it. "Every word is true, cupcake."

I crash my lips over hers, and she meets me right there. Her tongue flirts with mine. Her teeth graze over my mouth while I detonate over her with all of the passion—all of the assurances that my words couldn't even begin to touch. Rox has to know how much I care about her. After a lifetime of feeling unimportant, unwanted, invisible, I want to be the one to make her feel special. I want to show her that two people who care about one another more than anyone else on the planet can be magic. That it's so much more than a one-night stand, so much more than an entire string of girls I can hardly remember. Sex had become a thing, something like a chore that I penciled into my weekends to help pass the time because I promised my father I would shop around. I'm sure if I could rewind that conversation, I would have heard things a little bit different. I'm sure what he was trying to convey was look for someone special, someone who makes your heart thump like a jackhammer, who's spirit is so damn sweet you want to protect her every day for the rest of your lives. I finally found that person in Roxy. And I plan on protecting and loving her for the rest of my damn life. I only wish my dad was around to meet her. I'd love to be the one to tell him I didn't have to shop around anymore, that I found the one I've been looking for all along.

I reach down and run my hands inside her sweater, her warm skin heating my palms. Roxy's kisses taste like watermelon, like a bright spring morning with the hope of something new just on the other side. A horrible winter had passed, and, now, with Roxy in my life, every day is sunshine and roses.

Her kisses track up my neck until she takes a hard bite out of my ear.

I give a little roar, and she laughs. I know that's what she was after, hearing me scream.

"The first time I saw you"—she pants—"I had a mini orgasm just looking at you. I thought *who the hell does this guy think he is looking so damn hot?* You ruined me right then."

"Ruined." I unbutton her jeans and work them down along with her panties. "I like where you're going."

"I like where *you're* going." Her teeth glitter through her smile. I'd give anything to see her face light up more

ADDISON MOORE

often, and if it takes me pouring out my affection on her, I'm more than willing to repeat the effort on a daily basis.

"Anyway"—she sighs, tugging down my jeans and pulling my dick free from my boxers like rescuing an animal from captivity—"I wanted you in the worst way. I thought the only way I could have someone like you was in my dreams, and, trust me, we had a few adventures there, too."

I pluck the condom from my back pocket, and she takes it from me, tearing it open with her teeth.

"And here we are"—she holds the small rubber disc in the air like a prize—"with you on top of me, right where I've secretly wanted you from the beginning."

"Cole Brighton at your service ready and willing to make all of your fantasies come true." I float my fingers softly over her belly down to that heated slick between her thighs and glide over her.

Roxy gives a guttural moan as her body moves beneath me. Her eyes flutter into the back of her head as she takes in a breath and locks it in her throat.

"That mini orgasm you had when you first saw me?" I run my tongue over her mouth, and her lips open wanting more. "I want to apologize for that. It should have been much more pronounced. Honestly, I'm disappointed in myself. Let me make it up to you." My fingers move over her wet spot until she's gasping for air, her eyes opening every now and again with surprise.

"Look at me," I whisper right over her lips.

Roxy's lids flutter open. Her mouth parts just enough, and it takes far more restraint than possible for me not to kiss her.

"I want to see you come."

Her eyes widen a moment as if she were embarrassed.

"Well, then"—she rolls the rubber over me in less than two seconds—"turnabout's fair play." Roxy guides me in, and my eyes squeeze shut as I take in the sensation.

"Damn, you're so fucking tight."

"Look at me," she says it harsh like a reprimand. "I want to see *you* come." A tiny smile digs into the side of her cheek.

But I don't have some smartass comeback. There's not one coherent sound that can possibly make its way out of my throat. Instead, it takes all of my energy to keep my lids from sealing themselves shut. I stare down at Rox, at those bright-as-hell flashlights she sees the world through, those pillow-soft lips of hers blow out the softest vanilla scented breath, and I start to lose it. My fingers do their best to bring her right there with me, and I hold out until her head is moving in ecstasy, her breathing is erratic.

"Eyes on me." I hardly grunt out the words.

Rox looks back up at me, her pupils dilated into twin black pools so deep and terrifyingly beautiful, I jump right in with my soul. Our future is buried in that expectant look in her eye, and I'll do everything possible not to fuck it up.

We hold onto one another's gaze like climbing Everest with threadbare rope. We don't blink, falling faster, deeper.

Then it happens, her body bucks into mine, and I tremble over her in a fit of delirium like I have never known before.

"I love you, Cole Brighton." She pants into my ear, hot and breathy.

"I love you, cupcake." I press a wet kiss over her lips, her body still vibrating into mine. "I won't ever let you forget it."

She gives a hard sniff into my neck, and I pull back to find the moon highlighting a sheet of tears washing over her face. I don't say a word, just kiss each one while Roxy holds on like she's about to blow away.

I want to spend each day showing her just how special she is, just how much I love her. And I plan on spending my life doing just that.

Roxy has breathed new life into my world. I hope I can return the favor. I hope I can heal all the hurt buried deep inside her.

She's already healed mine.

11

All-Purpose Faking Mix

Roxy

School sucks per usual, and I bake my ass off all week, so I don't even pay much attention to the fact that with each passing day Aiden and his silicone squeeze have let an entire student body come to rest between them in our Entrepreneurship and Small Business class. I take a seat in my usual spot, and Aiden has the nerve to plop down beside me.

"What the hell do you want?" I grunt as I pull out my laptop and reading glasses. For the life of me, I don't know why he'd want to sit next to me unless he feels the sudden urge to have my boot hiked up his ass. And, believe you me, I would love to arrange that.

"LeAnn broke things off with me."

She cuts a look over to us when he says it and sneers at me for a minute.

"Crap." I spike up and trot over to her end of the room before falling into the seat beside her. The last thing in the world I want the teen queen to think is that I stole *her* boyfriend. God knows she'd take it out on me during the Sticky Quickie baking competition, and Melanie's ridiculous sexed-up muffins would run away with the cash and prizes. I'd do the same if the oven mitts were on the other foot—*hand*, whatever.

"What are you doing here?" She slits it out low, genuinely pissed. "Spying?"

A huff of a laugh escapes me "Right. Like I would ever side with a low life like Aiden Ryerson. He's lower than low. In fact, there isn't a snake lower than that bonehead." Okay, so I might have laid it on a little thick, but I still think someone like LeAnn needs it painted crystal clear. "We sisters need to band together and steer clear of sewage like him. We should send a mass email to every female in Hollow Brook, alerting them to his slimy ways." On the other hand, maybe I shouldn't have painted him to be such an asshole? The odds are still pretty good the two of them will be knocking boots by midnight, and then she'll be virally pissed at me for cutting down *her* man. "I mean, if you feel like that. I guess he's all right as long as he's treating you well." Not that Aiden couldn't "treat her well" *and* cheat on her, I should know first hand.

"He's pond scum. I caught him with Jeanie Waters in his dorm last week, and he thinks I'm going to let him weasel himself back into my life." Her lips quiver like she might cry. She's talking a good game, but the pain is right there underneath, bubbling to the surface in a way that I'm all too familiar with.

Jeanie Waters is Whitney Briggs go-to skank—much like Cole was our go-to manwhore.

"Don't even go there. He's so not worth the waterworks." I rub her back a moment. "Trust me, I know how much it sucks to have someone cheat on you." The professor steps into class, and the room quiets down to whispers. "If you ever need anyone to talk to, just find me. I'll be glad to listen." And, in an odd way, I mean it.

"You don't hate me?" Her eyes round out in surprise.

"Nope. I don't hate you." In fact, I should write her a thank you note for allowing me to make my way to Cole.

"I guess my mama was right." She slides down in her seat, her boobs buoying up to her chin like floatation devices. "There isn't a man on this planet who isn't capable of cheating."

An unexpected image of Cole rolling around in bed with Jeanie Waters comes up uninvited, and my stomach does a revolution.

Cole would never do that to me.

Would he?

ℬↈℭ

The sky churns the color of black licorice while the wind blows over me with its icy peppermint breath. I spot Baya inside Hallow Grounds and make my way over.

"Roxy!" She gives a brief wave.

"Hi girl." I grab a seat while Baya clears half her stuff off the table.

"No, that's okay. I have to get baking. The contest is set for Friday. I need to practice making my I Love Cole Brightons." I wrinkle my nose. I think I'll spare her the new-and-improved name for now. I'm pretty sure the mention of me sleeping with her brother is enough to make her rethink that cake pop she's twirling between her fingers. "That's kind of the name of my signature cupcake."

Her features soften as that smile fades from her face.

Crap. I swear if Baya says one negative thing about my relationship I'm going to start throwing lattes across the room.

"I heard." She pulls her lips in a line, no smile. "I also heard you weren't speaking to Laney or Ryder."

"I've just been busy." Each and every time they've called. "Okay, so I'm blowing them off, but if someone was trying to tell you that Bryson was just a flash in the pan, you'd cut them off at the balls, too. Cole loves me, and I feel the same."

"I get it." She holds up a hand in defense. "But I also get what Laney was trying to say."

"*What*?" A bite of heat sears through me. This is rich. Now Baya is going to throw her own brother under the bus? Wow, just fucking wow.

"Let me explain."

"Please, do. I'm dying to hear it."

"Laney doesn't really know Cole, *and* all she does know doesn't exactly put him in the best light." Baya leans into me, and I feel a little relief that she went in that direction. "She just doesn't want you to get hurt."

"*You* know Cole. We could gang up on Laney and yell at her until she realizes she's being ridiculous about this whole thing." Cole would never hurt me in a million years the way Aiden did.

"Yes"—she pauses with her hands stretched in front of her like a cat rousing from a long nap—"about that."

Crap.

"Cole has always been"—she twirls her fingers in the air searching for words—"how do I put this? A free spirit."

"I'm a free spirit," I snip. "Cut to the chase."

Baya cringes as if she were fearful, and she probably should be. "Look, Cole has always loved the ladies. I've just never seen him with one girl for very long. Quite honestly, he's impressing the shit out of me."

"Wait a minute." I jump back in my seat. "Are you telling me you didn't think we'd last?"

"I never said that," it speeds out of her. "Cole is just really growing as a person right now, and I'm glad it's with you. If anyone can tame Cole Brighton it's Roxy Capwell." She toasts me with her latte before taking a sip.

"What the hell is that supposed to mean?"

"It means it's going to take someone special to break him in. And, by the looks of things, that person is you." Her brows rise and fall. A look of apprehension washes over her face as if she's not entirely sure it's true.

Oh, holy hell.

If Baya doesn't have faith in Cole and me, why should I?

Do we really have any hope of pulling this off?

I can feel those dark clouds rolling in over my head once again, and I don't like it one fucking bit.

ভেত্তে

It's five o'clock and pitch dark by the time I finally make my way back to the apartment.

The scent of onions and peppers permeates the air, and there's a plume of white smoke coming from the kitchen.

"Hey, cupcake." Cole switches off the stove and brings a frying pan brimming with searing vegetables over to the table. It's only then I notice the surface has been cleared of its usual clutter, and the table is neatly set for two with a candle lit in the center.

"Wow." I plunk my stuff down in the corner and magnetize to him. "I can't believe you did all this."

"I wanted to." He lands a sweet kiss over my lips that I wish all the haters in the world could witness. "You hungry?"

"Just for you." I drive my tongue into his mouth and pull his body in tight to mine.

He moans into me. "Dinner can wait." Cole wrestles off my clothes, and I do the same until we hit just enough levels of undress to make things interesting. Cole sits down on the chair and pulls me over him with my legs wrapped on either side of his body.

His fingers flirt with my bra, and I pull his hand up and take a gentle bite of his pinky.

"Baya doesn't think we'll last either." I sag into him. I don't know why I brought it up other than the fact it kills me not to have her support.

"She said that?" His brows narrow in, serious as shit.

"Not those exact words, but, yes, she said that. I swear I don't get it."

Cole pulls me in by the back of the neck until his lips land over my forehead.

"I don't get it either. I'm sorry."

"Don't be." I take the small foil packet from him and roll on the condom. "I like proving people wrong." I just wish we didn't have to do it. It would have been great being couple friends with Laney and Baya of all people.

I straddle Cole and guide him in slowly.

His head knocks back. His eyes shut tight as he lets out a slow even breath like a train edging its way to the station.

"*Rox.*" My name rasps from his lips, and it sounds like heaven—*hell,* Cole feels like heaven. I let myself slip further down his body and soak it in as he fills me. It feels beautiful, *right*—and not one part of me is the slightest bit paranoid that this isn't going to last just short of eternity.

"I love you," I whisper into his ear, and, to my surprise, it comes out more of a question.

"Love you, too, Rox." He digs his fingers into my hips and guides me over him rough and needy until it feels as if I'm slamming my body over his, and, in truth, I am. I pull my head back and close my eyes. It feels as if I'm on some wild ride, as if I've accidently launched myself into space and am being jolted around the universe at a million miles an hour. My insides beg for relief. My heart hammers along with the shock of our bodies gyrating in time. With each plunge I can feel his need, his wanting, his desire to have me harder and faster than the time before.

A sharp cry comes from my throat as I begin to lose it. I steady myself over his shoulders as he pulls me in. Cole and I throb over one another in perfect ecstasy. We're in sync, and that's all that matters.

He brushes his lips over my ear. "It's me and you against the world, cupcake."

"We can take 'em." I tweak my fingers over his ribs and kiss him with a smile.

I hope we can take 'em.

We had better.

Cole

In the morning I wait until Roxy takes off for class before heading out. I give a couple brisk knocks on Baya and Bryson's door and wait a few minutes. I pound another round with my fist before Bryson shows his ugly mug, bedhead and all.

"Dude." I give a knuckle bump before heading inside. The air is stale, and Baya comes stumbling out from the hall with her hair rumpled into a bird's nest, wearing nothing but one of Bryson's old Black Bear T-shirts.

"What's up?" She heads over and offers me a quick hug. The sharp bite of body odor takes over, and suddenly I want to bolt before I'm introduced further to their bedroom antics. "Why are you here so early?"

"It's eight. Don't you have class?"

"Not till ten." She closes one eye as if she's still adjusting to the light. "Want some coffee?" She heads to the kitchen.

"Sure." I sock Bryson in the arm. "You mind if I talk to Baya alone?"

"Not a problem. I'll get lost in the shower for a while." He walks over to Baya and hugs her from behind, lands a kiss on her ear before whispering something in it.

Baya giggles as they part ways, and Bryson clears out of the room.

"It's nice to see you happy," I say, taking a seat at the counter. "Do you want to see me happy?"

"What's that supposed to mean?" She comes over as the coffee starts to percolate, and the scent of roasted grounds fills the air.

"It means, what the hell did you say to Roxy yesterday that made her so sick?"

Baya lets out a groan, dropping her head into her hands. "Really? Was she that upset?"

"Yes, she was that upset, and, by the way, you're the last person either one of us thought we'd have to defend our relationship to."

"I'm sorry." She bites down on her lip as she slides in next to me. "I swear to you, I didn't mean anything by it."

"What exactly *did* you say?"

"I said that I've never seen you so devoted to anyone before. That if there was anyone who could tame you, it was her."

"Tame me?" Crap. I grind my eye into my palm a moment. "Look, keep the commentary to yourself next time. Did you know Laney and Ryder gave her shit?"

She hides behind her hands a moment. "Yes," she squeaks. "I'll tell you what. You continue to be on your best behavior, and I'll talk to Laney. I'm sure we can work this whole thing out. We only want the best for the two of you,

ADDISON MOORE

and, most of all, no one wants to see either one of you with a broken heart."

"I'm not leaving her, Baya. You can relax. And I have no plans on breaking anybody's heart."

"I didn't say you'd be the one to do it."

I blink back, caught off guard. "What's that supposed to mean?"

"It means don't forget to give her space to heal. She's been burned pretty bad by that Aiden guy. Sometimes the next relationship can feel a little like a rollercoaster. I just don't want to see either of you bottom out. She's your first real girlfriend, Cole. Take it easy with her. She's more fragile than you know."

Baya pours us both a cup of coffee.

Take things slow.

The last thing I want to do is slow things down with Roxy and me. We're already cruising a million miles an hour into the stratosphere. What could be so bad about that?

But what goes up must come down.

Or maybe it doesn't.

Baya's right, this is all new to me.

I down the java juice just as Bryson comes back smelling like an Irish spring morning and head on out.

No sooner do I get out the door, I get a text.

Holy shit.

It's a picture—a chest shot of a very naked, very cold girl.

A greasy smile spreads across my face then glides off just as fast when I read the name at the top.

This isn't Rox.

It's Angel.

৪০০৪

I head over to campus and spot Laney up ahead. Perfect. I whistle over to her, and she turns around just as I glide beside her on my skateboard. If I can talk some sense into both Baya and Laney before noon, this will be a stellar day. Hell, maybe if I whip out my superhero cape, I might even tackle her brother.

Her eyes skirt the periphery of the student body before settling on mine.

Crap. This is going to be tougher than it looks. It's obvious Laney thinks I'm a dick.

"I want to apologize about last night." I hear the words stream from my lips, and I'm not even sure I believe them.

She folds her arms across her chest. "And what exactly are you apologizing for?"

"For giving you any impression that I might hurt Roxy." There, something cohesive came from my lips that

ADDISON MOORE

actually nails down exactly what has her worried most. I know she fears me hurting Rox because, deep down, I did too in the beginning, but I'm over that. Roxy and I are meant to be together. I've been with countless girls, and not one of them had the ability to make me feel the way she does.

Laney slits her eyes into mine like she means business. "You do realize that if you her hurt her, Roxy is going to be the least of your worries."

"Got it." I swallow hard. "I promise I have only the best intentions. I know what my history looks like, and I'm glad you're watching out for her, especially after what that asswipe did. But I'm not like that, I swear."

"Actions speak louder than words."

"What's that supposed to mean? I've been nothing but nice to Roxy."

"Nice to Roxy. Nice to Melanie. Nice to Carly. Nice to Jen, and Sophie, and Emma and—"

"Okay, okay, I get it. I've been around the block."

"You've been around *every* block." She throws her hands in the air, and, for a second, I think she's going to deck me. "Just keep your boy parts to yourself. Or better yet, restrict yourself to just one girl." Her forehead creases as she gives a brief look around. "Roxy can come across tough as nails, but the truth is she's—"

"Soft as a cupcake. I know." I cinch my backpack over my shoulder. "Rox and I are good. She's mine, and I plan

244

SUGAR KISSES

on keeping her that way for as long as she'll let me. I swear to you if I hurt her in any way, I'll give you full permission to kick my ass. I'll even bend over and make it easy for you." I hold my hands up. "I swear."

Laney gives a hard sigh as if she were giving in. "Okay. Just know if you blow this, the only one you're really hurting is the girl you claim to love. Be extra good to her, and I'll be your biggest cheerleader."

"Done." I hold out my hand, and she gives it a shake. Laney takes off, and I skate over to my first class just as I get a text.

I glance down. Another picture pops up uninvited—Angel. This time she's got her wings spread wide, and, holy shit, is this is even legal to send?

I delete the picture as fast as I can.

It looks like I'll have to do something drastic to get rid of my least favorite cling-on. I'll see if Bryson has any good tips. In the meantime, my non-response will have to be enough.

What the hell is wrong with that girl?

What the hell is wrong with everyone?

12

Sweetened Condensed Bullshit

Roxy

The Valentine's benefit needs you. I implore you to reconsider—if not for me, for your own future. So many of my friends have inquired about your services. Please respond and let me know either way. Sincerely, your mother.

I'm not sure which is more ridiculous, the fact my mother probably spent a small eternity composing a text that reads like a jury summons or the fact I've just sunk ten minutes staring at it.

"Oh, hell," I mutter.

Cole rolls over in bed and pulls me in. "Oh, hell, right back at you." He bleeds out one of his sexy grins, and I melt into him.

"Just a sec."

OK. I text back.

"There." I hand him the phone so he can read my mother's plea for cupcakes at her country club shindig. "Now at least I can say I'm doing whatever it takes to succeed in business."

"That you are. I'll help with whatever you need."

I roll into him and look up at his early morning stubble, his brows as they fan out and threaten to leap off his face.

"You're too good to be true."

"You're too good to be true." He presses his fingers over my thighs. "You ready for today?"

The open-air concert LeAnn is putting on for the school takes place this afternoon.

I pull back the curtain just above my bed only to meet up with a blade of sunshine spearing me in the eye. Yesterday it rained buckets, and, here, today it's a brilliant spring morning.

"God, even the weather is good to her. Some people catch all the green lights in life."

"And some people"—he buries a kiss in my neck—"get to wake up with Roxy Capwell by their side."

"Or Cole Brighton," I purr, tracking my finger down his chest, lower still to the base of his happy trail. "How about we start this day off right?"

"We already did." Cole sears a mouthwatering kiss over my lips. "We woke up in each others arms. It can only go up from here."

"Speaking of up." I land my hand on his overeager fifth appendage. "I like the way your lower half says good morning."

"It's easy when he likes what he sees." Cole sinks his hand to my thigh before tracking up and gently pressing a finger deep inside me, his mouth never leaving mine. He pulls on a condom and dips his leg between my knees. "You know what his favorite part is?"

"Are we still talking about your dick in third person?" A soft laugh bubbles from my chest. "'Cause I kind of like that, but my vagina sort of feels left out of the conversation."

"By all means invite her to join us. She's a special part of my life, and I'd hate for her to miss out."

"She says thank you, and she's dying to know what Harry's favorite part is."

"Harry?" His eyes enlarge into perfect green orbs.

"I think he deserves a name."

"Then Sally deserves one, too."

"*Sally?*"

"Yeah, it's only natural, right?"

"Very funny. Let me guess, Harry wants to meet Sally."

"Yes, but first—" Cole scoots in until our bodies fuse together at the chest, hot and sticky from a long night of setting the sheets on fire. Personally, I'm shocked Harry and the low riders have any more ammo to blow. "Harry wants to let you know his favorite part."

"What's that?" I nuzzle into him. Something about this cheesy conversation is heartwarming, and I want it to continue forever, well past noon and LeAnn's vocal contribution to the student body.

"It's being deep inside you." Cole bears those green lanterns into mine. "It's my favorite part, too." He touches his nose to my cheek a second. "I love how close it makes us feel, no pun intended. I feel alive, and happy, and a few feelings I didn't even know existed until I met you."

"Cole." I glance down a moment, my cheeks filling with heat. "I feel the very same way. You know what else?" I reach up and gently graze over his earlobe, trapping it between my teeth until he moans. "Each time you're in me it feels like the first time." It's true. I think of how lucky I am to have gorgeous Cole Brighton all to myself, and I die a little because, deep down, I'm still waiting for the other shoe to drop. Nothing has ever worked out for me, so why should this?

God, I hope I'm wrong.

Cole crashes his lips to mine. His tongue launches in on an exploratory effort that would put most cartographers to shame. He's memorizing the lay of the land, claiming my body for himself.

"Guess what?" he whispers into my mouth, and a heated shiver rises up my spine. "Harry wants to meet Sally."

I pull my knees up to either side of him, and he pushes in, slow at first before giving a full thrust, and a small cry gets caught in my throat.

I couldn't think of a better way to start the day off, or end the night, or kill time in the afternoon.

Cole Brighton can have me every day in every way.

But a part of me still wonders if this is too good to be true.

ॐ⊙ॐ

The I Slept with Cole Brighton cupcake is the very same recipe I created the morning after the first time we slept together, so it holds more than a slight sentimental appeal.

I take in the student body of Whitney Briggs as they gather around for the non-nutritional feast both Melanie and I provided. I can't help but smile when I see the words *I Slept with Cole Brighton* printed in bold red font on a banner above the monolithic display that LeAnn's "team" created to house the cupcakes. It took Cole, Bryson, Baya and me four trips to haul everything over on tiered carts we borrowed from the cafeteria.

The concert is just about to get underway as the student population swarms the frosted confections.

"Boy"—Melanie pops up beside me—"the way the sorority girls are attacking your cupcakes, you'd think a mini Cole Brighton is buried in each one." She twitches her nose. "I sort of wish he were!" She chortles a laugh that's quickly drowned out by LeAnn and her ability to slap a microphone with her hand to test its eardrum splitting capabilities.

"This is dedicated to the love of my life." Her voice carries across the field and into the forest that skirts the property. "Aiden Ryerson!"

My stomach drops.

"Crap." I knew I shouldn't have talked smack about him in class the other day. Now she's going to dock me points at next week's competition just because I cut down her boyfriend. And didn't she say he cheated? What the hell is she putting up with that for? Wait—why the hell did *I* put up with that? I'd never put myself through something like that again—once a cheat, always a cheat. Sally and I have no time for that kind of bullshit anymore.

"Looks like Cole just opened a kissing booth." Melanie nudges me with her shoulder.

I turn just in time to catch a familiar-looking blonde with her legs wrapped around his waist, her mouth planted firmly over his, and she's *kissing* him, right here in the open like he's fair-market game.

"What the hell?" I take a step toward him, and Melanie pulls me back by the elbow.

"You didn't know?" Melanie tries to campaign for my attention, but my eyes are firmly planted on Cole as he helps the skank with an ungraceful dismount and holds her at arms length.

That's better. I can't believe she just attacked him like that. Obviously, I need to go over and start wielding some mean Martial arts skills just to keep the girls from trying to climb my boyfriend.

"Know what?" I'm only vaguely interested in whatever lie she's ready to spew my way.

"Angel and Cole have a thing."

"They don't have a thing. Cole and *I* have a thing." Harry and Sally have a thing, but Cole and Angel do *not* have a thing.

"Well, sorry to be the one to break it to you, but Angel says they're messing around. She's all the time shooting him pictures of herself. I know for a fact she's taken a few tasteful selfies if you know what I mean." She gives a quick wink. "What the hell am I saying? They were tasteless as the day is long. She's my roommate, so I've played photographer a time or two. It's really kind of sick."

My stomach turns. Cole hadn't mentioned anything about naked selfies being delivered daily. Is that the kind of thing a boyfriend should fess up to? I have no clue because I've never been in an honest relationship before. And that's what we have, right? An honest relationship.

"Thanks for the info." I walk away and stumble into a body.

"Hey, sis." Ryder gives a sheepish grin. "Can you spare a hug for your big bro? I'm not liking the cold shoulder too much." His dark hair stains the stale grey sky as he gives me those puppy dog eyes. I could never stay mad at my brother for long.

"Done." I pull him into a tight embrace and take in his familiar cologne. Ryder has worn the same scent for as long as I can remember, and it feels safe holding him like this, familiar. I peek over his shoulder at Cole, and, dear God, there's an entire line of girls snaking around my cupcake booth waiting their turn with him.

"He *did* open a kissing booth." I watch as girl after girl runs up and gives him a lengthy, touchy feely, ass squeezing, cheek kissing, embrace. "Shit," I seethe.

"I wouldn't get too worked up." Ryder turns and inspects the scene with me. "From what I hear, they're all pretty psyched to have played a small part in his crowning cupcake glory." His chin dips as he looks into me. I can tell he's holding back the *I told you so.* "They think it's an ode to his one-night stand hotness." Ryder gives a dull smile that reads more like an apology just as Laney springs up beside him.

"Hey, girl." She ducks a little as if I might hit her simply for taking up the same air space as me. "You still hate me?"

"Only on days that end in W."

"Ha, ha." She pulls me in, and soon we're all engaging in some sort of awkward group hug. "Congratulations. Your cupcakes are a huge hit. I just had one, and I feel compelled to tell Cole how orgasmically beautiful it was." She touches her hand to her chest, and spontaneous tears sparkle in her eyes as if she were truly moved.

Only a thespian like Laney can pull off a move like that.

"So what are you going to do with your winnings? You know you're going to own this competition. Not one of Melanie's Ecstasy Delights are missing."

"Ten thousand dollars." I shake my head. I think I'm going to sock it away until graduation. As soon as WB puts that degree in my hand, I'm scouting for real estate. I'm going to open a storefront and hit the ground running.

A pair of arms embrace me from behind. "You've already hit the ground running, girl!" Baya twirls herself around my body as if I had morphed into a striper pole. "I'm telling you, we're going to rock those judges faces off. I can't believe Cole and I get to be there to watch you win."

"You're going to *help* me win. You both will." I turn to look at Cole, and all I see is a mob of girls with cell phones raised above their heads, documenting his every move. All those girls seem far too happy to see him. I bet they'd love to see him in action again, and just the thought makes my stomach pinch with jealousy. I hate this feeling. I hate being the girl who suddenly feels as if she's walking on the razor's edge of her relationship with nothing but the sheer cliff of a breakup to the right and left.

"And now"—LeAnn's voice bellows over the student body, popping and cracking through the speakers like a firecracker—"I'd like to sing a song with the love of my life. Honey bear, come on up here."

I watch as Aiden climbs on stage with the look of complete admiration in his eyes while gazing at her. He never once looked at me that way, and now it makes sense. He never loved me. I wasn't the one for him.

"We're gonna sing a little duet," she belts the words out into his face. "Don't go breaking my heart, baby."

They start in, and, surprisingly, Aiden doesn't sound half bad. The old me would have prayed for rain—for the stage to electrify and jolt the two of them into kingdom come in a spectacular shower of sparks and fire, but the new me doesn't give a rat's ass that they're burping out the lyrics to some quasi-breakup song together. Instead, I turn back to Cole, back to his happy harem ready and willing to get on their knees for him.

Will I ever be enough for someone like Cole?

Or, more importantly, will I ever feel like enough?

Cole

Angel updated her status on all social networks to read, *in a relationship with Cole Brighton* then sent me the links.

"What the hell?" I stare at my phone in disbelief.

Roxy said she was going to grab a cup of coffee with Baya and Laney after the concert, so I head back to the apartment alone.

I step into the elevator and ride up just as another text comes in—a picture of Angel and me at the concert.

Shit. I must have smiled for a thousand pictures out there, but for this one I wish I would have pulled my T-shirt up over my face.

I step out onto my floor with my finger ready and willing to hit delete when I spot Bryson just outside his door with Baya and head over.

"Need your thoughts on something, bro, if you got a minute." I nod at Bryson before turning to my sister. "Rox is waiting for you at Hallowed Grounds."

"She is?" Baya looks stumped by the idea.

"Yeah, she said she was grabbing coffee with you and Laney. I guess she wants to decompress. This was a pretty big day for her."

"She didn't mention it." Baya unlocks their door. "And I doubt Laney is there. She said she felt a cold coming on.

I'm pretty sure Ryder took her home. She's got a big audition coming up, and she doesn't want to blow it."

I pause a moment.

"I must have heard her wrong." But I know I didn't. Why would Roxy make something like that up?

"So what's going on?" Bryson motions me into their apartment.

"There's this girl."

"Oh, shit." Baya seethes. "So help me God if you're even thinking of dumping Roxy for greener vaginal pastures—"

"Relax." I cut her off before she can get going. Once Baya starts up, it's impossible to stop her. "Nobody is dumping anybody. I've got some psycho chick that's been hounding me for months, and I have no freaking clue how to get her off my back."

"*Oh.*" Baya perks up. "That's a different story. Who is she?"

"Some chic from Alpha Chi named Angel. When I slept with her, I had no clue she was a virgin, and it's just escalated from there. She's sent me nude pictures—spread eagle and shit."

Baya's eyes bug out. "Does Roxy know?"

"No, I deleted them hoping that nutcase would knock it off. But it's only gotten worse. She declared me her boyfriend and plastered a picture of us all over the internet."

"Dude." Bryson shakes his head. He snatches his wallet and phone off the counter and nods toward the door. "Let's do this, man. Let's head to Alpha Chi and pay her a visit. No use in postponing the inevitable."

"Let's do it."

Bryson kisses Baya goodbye, and we head out.

"It's like old times, just me and you."

"Old times." I shake my head. "No offense, but I wouldn't go back for anything."

"Yeah." Bryson gets that goofy grin on his face like he does when Baya is around. "I wouldn't go back for anything either."

萃鑧

Alpha Chi is lit up like a pumpkin. Red tinsel hearts hang in each window as a reminder to the male population that Valentine's Day is in a week. Of course, I didn't forget. This will be my first with Roxy, and I plan on making it special. I'm sort of low on cash, so a visit to Tiffany's is out, but I should have enough for dinner and a movie.

I pause walking up the steps to the sorority.

"Oh, shit," I whisper.

"No backing out now." Bryson yanks me up the steps by the elbow.

"I just realized I haven't touched the inheritance from my dad's life insurance policy. It was mine the day I turned twenty-one, and I can cash out anytime I want."

"Cool. Now let's go break some hearts. I'll even let you treat me to a burger after."

"Sorry, sweetheart, but my dance card is filled. I need to reward Roxy for using me as her muse."

Bryson gives a gentle knock to the door, and a short blonde answers. Before we know it, we're inundated with screaming girls, chanting, *I slept with Cole Brighton!*

Bryson shakes his head at the melee. "I'm not feeling the love."

I slap my hand on his shoulder. "Get over yourself, buddy. It's my time to shine." Angel pops up from behind the crowd and waves. "Suddenly I'm wishing I wasn't so damn shiny." I break my way through the crowd of screaming girls, with hands pawing over my body as if I were a rock star. Someone cups my crotch, and I jump.

"Watch the boys," I say as I make my way to Angel. "Can we go somewhere to be alone?" The entire sorority stills. An audible collective gasp circles the room, soon replaced with an adolescent string of *oohs*.

Angel straightens. Her chest pops forward with pride as if I had just tapped her to be my soul mate out of a sea of thousands. Crap. Maybe this wasn't Bryson's brightest idea.

We head to the kitchen where there's nary a soul. I pull up a seat at the counter and motion for her to take it.

"You're such a gentlemen," she sings over a string of giggles.

"I'm not really." I sit down next to her. "I came by tonight because I wanted to talk to you in person."

"Oh my, God!" Her hands shake as she covers her mouth. Tears instantly spring from her eyes. "*Yes!*"

"Yes?"

"Yes, I'll marry you!" She leaps from her seat to mine, and before I know it we're on the floor with about a dozen girls snapping pictures of us with their phones.

"No." I gently pull her off. "I came here to tell you it's over." There. If anything I've officially broken up with her in front of at least twelve of her sisters. "I'm sorry it had to come to this." I shake my head because I'm serious as shit. "I swear to you, I never set out to break your heart."

Her nostrils flare. Her eyes glitter up with tears, and I feel like a sack of shit on fire that's just begging to be stomped out of its misery.

"It's not true." She scoots back as one of her sisters pulls her to her feet. I get up and try to take a step toward her, but she backs away.

"It is true. I'm in love with Roxy Capwell, and I always have been." Okay, so maybe I didn't have to take it that far, but, swear to God, if she sends me a naked selfie in the morning, I won't regret digging in so deep.

"You're going to pay for this." Her eyes slit to nothing. Her chest heaves as she pants out the words. "I'll have to tell my dad, and now you'll be sorry you ever laid eyes on me!" She runs screaming out of the room, hysterical with tears.

"Fuck," I mutter. I'd do anything if I could rewind time, right back to my first day at Whitney Briggs, and stop the one-night stand train before it ever left the station.

I'd tell myself there was someone special coming soon that I would fall madly in love with and to hell with all those other girls.

The last thing I ever wanted to do was break anybody's heart.

13

Icing on the Cake

Roxy

After a long afternoon of listening to LeAnn warble out tunes, I finally crawl home, dog tired, both mentally and physically exhausted. Melanie donated the remainder of her Ecstasy Delights to the homeless shelter, and, well, there were none of my signature cupcakes left. It turns out that everyone who *did* sleep with Cole Brighton showed up and ate one.

I get off the elevator and head to my apartment just as Baya peeks her head out the door.

"Hi, Rox! I thought you were Bryson. I've got a shift at the Black Bear, and he's sort of my ride. Hey, was I supposed to meet you for coffee? Cole mentioned something about it."

"No. I ended up having coffee by myself. Sometimes a girl just has to clear her head." I note the door to my apartment is ajar. "Maybe Cole can give you ride?"

"He's not home either. He took off a few minutes ago. He said he needed to talk to some girl named Angel." Her fingers fly to her mouth a second. "Anyway, I'd better finish getting ready. And don't forget, I'm all yours next Friday. We're going to nail the competition to the cupcake-loving wall."

"Right." I pause a second before heading into the apartment. Angel? That's the girl that Melanie said he had a *thing* with.

I step into the entry just as a couple of girls spring out from Cole's bedroom. They tear open their matching white robes, showing off all of their God-given glory for the free world to see—or, more specifically, my boyfriend.

"*Surprise!*" They sing in unison.

"You're not, Cole." The blonde on the right whines as they both sag with disappointment. "Is he on his way?"

"What?" I snatch up granny's wooden spoon and chase them all the way to the door. "Come back here so I can properly knock some sense into you!" I shout as they bypass the elevator and head for the stairs.

"Tell him Tia and Mia came by!" They lose themselves in a giggle fit as they trot down the hall.

"Fucking skanks." I stumble over to the table and flip open my laptop. I need to relax, unwind, and loosen up. Of course, girls are going to look at Cole, *want* Cole. He's gorgeous. I scroll through my emails before hitting my roll call of social network sites and...oh, God. Clogging my Whitney Briggs social newsfeed is one picture after another of Cole and *Angel*? These were taken less than a half hour ago.

"Shit." I stare at the one of Cole and Angel headed out of the room captioned, *luckiest girl in the world.* Another one with them on the floor locked in one another's arms, *can't keep his hands off her.* The third is a video. I click on it and watch as Angel giggles over his body while writhing on the floor.

"Oh my, God!" Angel slaps her hand over her mouth. *"Yes!"*

"Yes?" Cole answers, surprised.

"Yes, I'll marry you!" Her face lunges toward his and the video cuts out.

"What the—"

The door shuts, and I glance up to find Cole standing there. "Hey, Rox."

"Are you getting married?" Words I thought I'd never say to my new boyfriend.

"What?" He swoops in and scans my laptop. "Shit. I can explain everything."

"Oh, fuck." I jump up and start grabbing crap at random and throwing it into a trash bag. "I'm out of here."

ADDISON MOORE

"No, wait." He snatches me by the arms and pulls me into him. "I'm not marrying anyone. I swear, I just went over to break up with her."

"You were seeing someone while you were *sleeping* with me?" I bark out an insolent laugh. "Boy, was I ever wrong about you." I break free from his stronghold and dash into my room to gather my things.

"I wasn't seeing her. She's obsessed with me. She's been sending me naked pictures and shit, and tonight she called me her *boyfriend,* so I went over to set her straight." He tries to block my path to the bathroom, but I circle around him. "Are you breaking up with me?"

"It would seem realistic."

"Roxy—she's fucking nuts. I swear there was nothing going on."

"Then why didn't you tell me all this?" I snatch my toothbrush and deodorant. I'll leave the tampons as a reminder of what he lost. Maybe he can shove one up his ass once in a while to remind himself of what a pussy he is. "Face it, Cole, you can't change. Everybody was right about you. This is never going to work. You just said you loved me to get in my pants!" I roar it in his face as I stumble out the door.

Thankfully Baya's apartment is unlocked, and I let myself in without knocking.

A gasp emits from the sofa. Baya jumps off Bryson and adjusts her clothes in a hurry.

"If you don't mind, I'll just hang out in your spare room for a few minutes—or days." I head over without waiting for a response. "My head feels like it's going to explode."

I wish it would.

⁂

All week I give Cole an icy shoulder. I told him point blank when we "accidentally" bumped into one another on Tuesday that I would kick him in the nads if he ever tried to speak to me again, so, suffice it to say, he's given me space. On Wednesday he started sending a mountain of text messages, and about six o'clock last night, I responded to a few with an entire slew of red-faced emoticons. That about sums up how I'm feeling—embarrassed and pissed to hell.

Lucky for me, there's been so much baking to do for my mother's Valentine benefit that I haven't had a lot of time to nurse a broken heart although I did eye the vanilla extract crooked a time or two, not that imitation bourbon could ever cure my blues. Nevertheless, I'm sure Holt or Bryson can whip up a Pink Panty Dropper for me at the end of this long weekend. God knows there's one bartender at the Black Bear I won't be dropping my panties for anymore or speaking to for that matter.

On the morning of the Sticky Quickie baking competition, I send Baya next door to gather a few of my necessary supplies. Mostly it's just my good luck charm, my granny's wooden spoon which I might have cast a pox on when I chased two naked girls from the apartment with it. Freaking Cole and his endless line of hussies. My heart sinks as I stand outside the door of the apartment I once shared with him. Why the hell did I have to fall so hard so fast?

Cole comes out into the hall, ignoring his sister's perky *good morning*.

He steps into me and settles his eyes over mine. A fire of lust lights up the tiny space between us, and every ounce of me is begging to close in the gap.

"Let me hold you," he says it sweet, quiet, like a dying man's final wish.

"Only if we win." Like it or not, I still need him. Ten grand is still on the line, and I'll need every red cent to get on my feet, post graduation. God knows there's not another soul I can trust to help me once I'm out in the real world.

"Oh my, God—*Cole!*" Baya wails from inside.

"Not now," he groans. His eyes soften as he steps in close. "Come inside with me, there's something I want to show you." His cologne saturates my senses. My entire body demands to lunge at him and crash my lips to his. Damn hormones.

"Let me guess, you've been saving all the condom wrappers you've burned through over the years and finally turned them into a collage? No thanks. Save the dick art for someone who cares."

"It's not that." He touches his finger to my cheek, his gorgeous face blooming with grief. "I swear if you just give me a minute I can make you understand. I'd love for you to step inside."

"Never," I snipe.

Baya comes out with my basket o' crap, and we make our way to the elevator.

"Be at the studio by one o'clock sharp," I yell it out to Cole like a threat as the elevator doors swoosh shut, and my heart shatters into a million irreplaceable pieces. The truth is, I don't want my heart put back together. It only beat for Cole, but I'll never admit it, deep down I know it always will.

"Oh, Rox." Baya shakes her head. "That boy loves you something fierce."

I lean against the cool steel of the elevator wall. "Yeah, well, he's got a funny way of showing it."

ଛଔଓଷ

By the time Baya and I arrive in downtown Jepson, the sky has traded in its perky blue hue for a dark layer of ominous purple clouds. Technically Baya didn't need to be here until later either but wanted to support me from start to finish.

We head into the kitchen studio where the competition will be broadcast from and meet up with the network liaison. It's a live show that's going to air on the local cable network, but I've been trying hard not to dwell on the fact thousands of people will potentially watch me freeze up in front of the camera and look like a doofus. The truth is I can't wrap my head around the competition right now. Instead I've been ruminating on my brief encounter with Cole this morning. There was something sweet in his eyes that said I need you, at least that's what I want to believe. They might have been saying *I covered the evidence from last night's romp pretty damn well! Maybe I should invite her inside and see if she notices*? Why the hell else would he want me to step into the apartment? Certainly he could have told me everything he wanted right there in the hall, like *I'm sorry* and *I'll burn my balls at midnight to prove it.*

Baya and I are led into an oversized auditorium where an endless string of stage lights hover above. The cameras are all neatly pointed at miles of bulky appliances, and the stainless kitchen facility is painted a cheery shade of blue.

"This is really happening!" Baya grabs my hands and jumps up and down like we've just won the lotto. "I can't believe this, Rox! You're hitting the big time!"

I glance around at the well-lit facility, the oversized glossy kitchen with its fancy stainless ovens and frown.

"Yeah, well, I guess it's all right." A part of me would much rather be baking in Cole's tiny apartment while he begs on his knees for my first batch discards. I'd probably lace them with arsenic, but that's beside the point.

"Just all right? Are you nuts?" She drags me over to the vast display of ingredients, and electric mixers big enough to fit a small car in. "This is baking nirvana! You're going to win this. Trust me"—she leans in just as Melanie Harrison walks in with one of her girls, the two of them clad in matching pink polos—"I've tasted her cupcakes. Ecstasy Delight? Not so much."

I give a little laugh just as the studio liaison comes by with a shit load of paperwork for me to fill out. The next few hours fly by, and, before I know it, they're cuing us into our respective positions.

Melanie trots over in her six-inch killer heels. I hope she cracks both ankles in half before the day is through.

"I guess it's you and me representing Whitney Briggs." She lets out a string of requisite giggles. The other two competitors are both from Ridgewood University, our crosstown rival. I guess if I didn't win, I'd rather it be Melanie, but I'm not feeling charitable enough to verbalize the sentiment.

"So it seems."

"May the best girl win." She offers up a knuckle bump, but I sneer down at her pasty-looking hand.

"Don't worry, I will." I cross my arms over my chest in the event she plans on standing there all day with her fist pointed at me. I'm feeling a little ornery toward girls who've slept with Cole Brighton. In fact, I'm thinking of changing the name of my signature cupcake to just that, I Hate Girls That Have Slept with Cole Brighton, which covers all girls in a twenty-mile radius—minus Baya and Laney. God, I'm back to hating people again. Isn't the planet about due for some mutant contagion?

The judges take their seats, and LeAnn gives me a little wave. I'd smile back, but I'm done with fake relationships.

Speaking of fake relationships, I can't help but note I'm down one assistant at the moment.

"Where's your brother?" I whisper to Baya. I'm pretty sure it's not cause for elimination to be one man down, but, holy hell, this will suck big hairy dicks if he doesn't show up quick.

"I don't know. I'll shoot him a text."

The host comes out with all the fanfare of the Oscars and does a little spiel before introducing us to our choice ingredient we're to integrate into at least one of the cupcakes we present to the judges.

"Please don't be fish, please don't be fish," I mutter to myself.

He plucks the tablecloth off the mystery mountain, and I swear, every girl in the room sighs with relief.

"The mystery ingredient is *fruit!*" he shouts, and everyone gives a gleeful clap, myself included.

"I can do this!" I spin into Baya—only she's not there anymore.

Crap.

The bell rings, and I run to the table and slap my hand over the pineapple at the exact same moment Melanie decides to unleash her crooked claw.

"It's mine, bitch!" She snakes it from beneath me and takes off running.

Shit.

The two skanks from Ridgewood grab a bunch of bananas and strawberries respectively. Double crap.

I reach for the kiwis and head to my table.

"Contestant number three, where is your team?" The host looks stunned with his manufactured smile, his doll-inspired hair plugs.

"In the bathroom." I glance at the darkened corridor that leads toward the facilities. I pray to God Baya makes it quick.

"Let's hope a little downtime on the throne is all that's needed." He starts to walk away then does a double take. "Where's your other assistant?"

"Also in the bathroom," I snip. "Let's hope a little downtime on the throne is all that's needed," I parrot back.

Great. I've all but let everyone in a tri-state area know that both Baya and Cole are constipated.

"Well, it looks like your competitor is down one man as well." He points the silly glitter-covered mike toward Melanie.

Ha! I didn't even notice she had a handicap. This is going better than I hoped.

I lose myself trying to do every job on the planet for the next half hour until it dawns on me that neither Baya nor Cole have managed to elbow up beside me.

I pluck my phone from my jeans. Crap. There's a text from Baya.

Emergency - had to leave. Won't be back. Sorry!

I sway in my shoes for a moment.

"What the heck?" Oh my, God, it's really happening. Everything I've ever wanted is slipping away. What the hell is wrong with me? Did I step on the last four-leaf clover as a child? Did I puke in a pot of gold at some all night kegger? Why is it that things can never go my way?

My entire body stings as if I were just bitch slapped by the universe because apparently I was.

"I can't believe this." I stagger from my table with the mixer still spinning, the ingredients laid out haphazard, the pound of kiwis taunting me as I pull away. "I'm not going to win."

There's no way in hell I can do this alone. I glance over at Melanie barking out orders to her single assistant, and I do the unthinkable—I head over.

Just because I'm out doesn't mean Whitney Briggs, is.

We bake our asses off for the next five hours straight and take this motherfucker all the way home.

The host hands Melanie a ten thousand dollar check, the size of a small refrigerator, and I shed a little tear.

It could have been mine.

And somewhere out there that rabbit foot I tossed in the trash back in fifth grade laughs.

Cole

"How many fingers am I holding up?" Bryson waves his hand over my face far too close for me to ever make out what the fuck he's holding, no less how many there are.

"Dude, get the hell away from me." My lips are so swollen it comes out like garbled bullshit. In fact, I would have much rather had my body gnawed on by a bunch of *bulls* until I literally turned into shit rather than have my ass kicked by a band of burly bikers.

"Do you remember what any of them looked like?" Baya is shaking, she's so frightened for me. I told Bryson not to call her, but he insisted. He said she'd kill him if he didn't. He's probably right, but I knew she'd come straight here, and, more importantly, I knew where she was at.

"No," I grumble, wincing as I sit up. "I stepped into the parking lot on the way to my truck, and there was some gorilla in a leather vest leaning against it. He dragged me behind the building, and"—I hold out my busted arm—"the ass kicking ensued. They all looked the same—big, hairy white dudes with combat boots. If you need to know a shoe size, I'm sure I've got a few imprinted on my back. I'm damn lucky to be alive. If Angel didn't come around the corner screaming, I don't know what would have happened to me."

Baya and Bryson exchange a quick look.

"What?" I moan reaching for the ice bag the nurse left on my bedside. "And, by the way, you can check me out of here. I want to go home."

Baya runs her fingers through my hair, and I try not to groan. "Not until the X-ray comes back for your arm."

"It's broken." I've had enough broken bones in my life to know, not to mention once the beast bent it far enough back, the clean snap gave it away—sounded like a tree limb cracking off.

Bryson turns on the television and fiddles with the remote until we land on a local channel that's hosting the baking competition.

Baya sucks in a lungful of air as she stares up at the screen.

"What's wrong?"

"It's Roxy. Her workstation is dark. The camera just panned right over it."

Crap. I knew I should have kicked Bryson in the balls when he went for the phone. Bryson just happened to step out of the building in time to see them hauling my sorry ass off in the ambulance.

"Look!" Baya jumps up and down, and we watch as Roxy works her magic in the kitchen. She's so damn beautiful, I have to fight the tears. God only knows what she's thinking right now. It's not until a half hour sweeps by do we even notice that she's rocking it out for the opposing fucking team.

"Shit." I pull the pillow over my head.

The doctor comes in and affirms my broken arm theory, and, before I know it I'm sporting a bright blue cast.

"We're going to keep you overnight for observation." He smiles down over his wire-rimmed glasses.

"Then what?" I ask, glancing at the screen for an update on Roxy.

"If you wake up, you get to go home." He nods at Baya and Bryson before leaving the room.

"Sounds like a plan." I nestle my head into the pillow and watch as Roxy bakes her ass off.

"You better wake up," Baya says it like a threat. Her eyes fill with tears, and I know that a part of her is experiencing the pain of losing our father all over again.

"Come here." I pull her into a partial hug, and it feels as if my ribs are snapping one by one. "I promise you, I'll wake up. Don't worry about me. I'm stealth." I turn off the light above my head as Bryson and Baya head toward the door. "Do me a favor, don't say anything to Roxy. I want to be the one to tell her."

"If she asks, I'm not lying." Baya glances at the floor a moment because we both know Roxy is probably too pissed to ask.

As soon as they take off, I close my eyes, and Roxy warbles in and out of my mind like a glass of water just out of reach. I'd give anything for her to be real—for her to be here. The tears start coming, and I try to swallow them back.

I wish my dad could have hung out a little longer on this planet. Not that he had a choice, but still. It would have been amazing to have him around for guidance and support. Mom worries too much, and I'm pretty sure she's the last person I'd go to with "girl" trouble. I sure wouldn't mind bringing Roxy home to meet her first chance I get. Hell, Mom will be out for graduation come May. I'd love for her to meet Roxy then. Of course, I'll have to point her out from a distance like a stalker. Maybe Baya can introduce her? At least that way Mom can meet the girl I gave my heart to.

A gentle knock erupts over the door, and I force my swollen eyes open. The shadow of a girl stands against the light of the nurses' station, and I struggle to make her out.

"Rox?" I sit up and groan as she comes into focus.

"It's just me." A blonde with a high-pitched voice waves at me—Angel.

Shit.

"I suppose I owe you a thank you." I force a smile to come and go. After all, she was the one who scared the fuckers away.

"For what?" Her eyes widen to the size of softballs. "I'm the one who put you here."

"Excuse me?" I blink a few times to make sure I'm not hallucinating, although at this point I wouldn't mind. I could really use some damn sleep. "I must have had my brains bashed in pretty good. I could have sworn you were the one who yelled for them to stop."

"I did." Her fingers touch at the tips as if she were nervous. "I didn't want you to get hurt." She pulls her shoulders to her ears and pauses. "And I didn't want my dad and his friends to get into any trouble."

"Why would your dad get into trouble?" I shake my head, and the room gives a spin.

She leans into me with the look of frustration building on her face.

"Oh, shit." I close my eyes and lean hard into my pillow. "Your dad is the one who beat the crap out of me." It all makes perfect sense now. "Great—I bet he's going to gather up more of his goons and come back to finish the job."

"No, he won't." She picks up the corner of the blanket and threads it through her fingers. "I made him promise to leave you alone. Once I ask him to do something, he does it." Her lips tremble. Her hands shake like an addict.

"You tell him to kick my ass?"

"Nope." She holds her hand up like a Girl Scout. "I swear, I thought he was just going to *talk* to you. He said, *don't worry baby, I'm just going to knock some sense into him,* and the rest...." She lets her words hang in the air.

"Crap," I moan. "I'm sorry I hurt you, Angel. But I think we're even now. You should probably go."

"So you won't rat out my dad?"

"Won't have to. The apartment building is loaded with security cameras. They already have a clear picture of every one of those guys, and if their bikes were around, they've got that, too. Trust me, I'm not looking for any more trouble. Just tell your old man I got the message. I won't be messing with his baby girl anymore. That's probably all he wants to hear."

"Will do." She turns to leave and pauses. "Cole? Do you hate me?"

"Nope. I don't hate you, Angel. I hate me for being such a jerk to begin with. I'm sorry about the way I treated you. Are we good?"

She gives a sheepish smile. "We're good."

I listen as her footsteps click all the way down the hall.

It takes another hour before I fall asleep. I dream all night long of Roxy, clad in leather, wielding a mean whip while dressed like the sexiest damn biker chick I've ever seen. She kicks my ass all night long, and I love every last beating.

I'd let her whip me to kingdom come if given the chance.

Hell, I'd beg for it just to be near her again.

14

Red Velvet Valentine

Roxy

Unbelievable.

The bastard didn't even call.

Late Saturday afternoon, Baya and Bryson help me load up a crap ton of cupcakes into the back of his truck and drive them over to the Valentine's benefit at the country club. Mom said lunch was included if we wanted to stay, so I put on my best black dress, complete with strategically placed slits running all the way down my thighs, and a pair of patent leather stilettos. I figure for the sake of Baya and Bryson, I can be a wallflower for one evening. Baya seems pretty psyched about the whole thing.

"You never know"—she pats my cheek as we roll in the final cart of cupcakes through the country club's kitchen—"your prince charming could be here tonight."

"Doubtful."

"Darling!" Mom trots over in her designer heels with her arms open wide as if she's actually happy to see me. "Your father is in Tokyo on business. He so wishes he could be here. Let me hold you, sweetheart. I've missed you," she whispers into my ear. "Goodness, you smell divine."

"So do you." Mom smells like an afternoon in Paris—always has, always will. Her hair is framed softer around her face with more blonde highlights mixed in. "Everything looks great." I glance around at the blanket of twinkle lights hanging from the ceiling, the long stem roses in every hue of red adorning the tables. "It looks perfectly romantic." I sniff back unexpected tears.

"I have a surprise for you." She presses her lips together. We have the same bone structure—same ears, too, but neither of us dares expose them for fear of giving up our true heritage as elves. "He's right around the corner. He brought a little guest with him that I think will be pleasing to you as well."

He? Could it be?

"Oh my, God." I suck in a quick breath and follow my mother, past a sea of bodies, over to the entry. "I can't believe he's really here," I whisper. My heart beats erratic. Begging my forgiveness at the country club in front of God and all of my mother's stuffy friends is one of the most romantic things Cole could do to apologize for his moronic behavior. I bet his truck stalled yesterday, or he got mobbed by an entire group of sexed-up coeds who took him by force to their sorority and tried to cage him in their walk-in closets as a love slave.

"He *is* here." Mom gives my fingers a squeeze, and, now, we can all be a family again. We clear a crowd of people and smack right into—Ryder and Laney?

Crap. Of course, she meant Ryder. She doesn't even like Cole—or Laney for that matter.

"What's going on?" I pull my brother into a quick hug. "*Hey.* Why aren't the two of you in Los Angeles? Don't you have an audition to get to?" It looks like my bad juju is rubbing off on everyone I love. "Let me guess, you missed the plane because of me."

"No. The audition was canceled." Laney swats me with her purse. "And, by the way, the entire world doesn't revolve around you." She presses her lips together tight like she might cry. "Except when it does. I heard about what happened yesterday." She wraps her arms around me and gives a great big rocking hug. "I'm so sorry."

"I wish I knew you guys were in town. I would have called you both to the studio." I pull back and take up Ryder's hand, too. "At least someone from Whitney took home the prize." I shrug it off. "The new me doesn't really care. I guess it just wasn't meant to be."

"The new you?" Ryder dips his chin.

"Yup. I'm a roll-with-the-punches kind of girl now. No more wishing the world would disintegrate in one big nuke explosion. I'm all for live and let live." And as long as I don't ever put my heart on the line again, I should be fine. I turn back to my mother. "So this is my surprise? You knew Ryder and Laney would be here?" Ryder and Laney swore off my mother last Christmas, so I'm getting psychological whiplash trying to figure out what the hell is happening.

"I invited them, and they graciously accepted my offer." Mom pauses to blink back tears. "I believe I owe everyone here an apology. Laney, I'm sorry I ever treated you so poorly. If you could find it in your heart to forgive me, I would love to have both you and Ryder back in my life." She turns to me. "Roseanna, same with you and Colon."

I'm momentarily thrown by the fact she thinks I'm dating someone named after a body part that specializes in excrement. On second thought...

"I accept." Laney lunges at her with a brief hug. "I don't like conflict, but I do love your son."

"And I love Laney." Ryder is quick to defend her. "In fact, we've made the decision to marry this June."

The room stills for a moment. Mom's jaw hits the floor then bounces up again.

"That's wonderful." She swallows a little of her pride but wisely so because whatever negative remark that was begging to pop from her mouth she was able to contain for once.

Damn. My mama has finally grown up.

"I'm proud of you, Mom." I pull her into a real hug, and, for the first time she hugs me back, *hard,* just the way granny used to.

"I'm proud of you, too, Roseanna." She pulls back and hitches my hair behind my ear. "Rumor has it, you make the most delicious desserts in town."

"I learned from the best." I give an impish grin. "Your mother."

That permanent frown melts from her face, and she softens. "She would've loved to have heard that."

I rest my head over her shoulder. "I'm sure she did."

"Can anyone join this party?" A familiar voice comes from behind, and I turn with a smile because I'm one hundred percent certain it's—

"Cole?" I take one look at him and gasp. I thought for sure I'd see the Cole I knew, not this battered and bruised version.

Holy shit.

He's welted along one side of his face. His lip is cut on the bottom, and his left eye is nearly swollen shut.

"God, who did this to you?" I rush into his arms, and it's only then I notice one of them is broken. "Is this why you weren't there yesterday?" I can't even breathe while looking at him.

"This is why."

Ryder steps in, his face rife with worry. "What happened?"

"I swear to God, Ryder, if you're responsible for this—" the words speed out of me like a bullet.

"He's not." Cole tightens his grasp around my waist. "Angel's father did it." He relays the story of the biker gang—crazy Angel, the psycho stalker chick that's been after him for months.

"I should have believed you in the first place. We could have left together for the competition, and this never would have happened."

"Not true. They were pretty determined." He pulls me in and lands a gentle kiss to my cheek. "In fact, I'm glad you were nowhere around."

Mom clutches at her pearls. "Have they apprehended these hooligans?"

"The cops came by the hospital before I left. Angel helped hunt down two of them." He glances over at me. "She texted and let me know she's transferring to Ridgewood. She's pretty sorry about how everything turned out."

"She's lucky she won't be around," I growl. "I'm not opposed to giving her a smack down of her own."

"Roseanna!" Mom's eyes pop, and I back down.

"Or a good talking to." I wrap my arms around poor, bruised Cole. "Speaking of talking to." I nod for Mom to say something nice to Cole. If he's going to be my boyfriend, she's going to have to get used to seeing him around.

"I'm very sorry you were hurt." She gives a long blink. "And I'm very sorry for the way I acted when we met a few weeks back. If my daughter likes you enough to keep you around, that's more than good enough for me."

"Really?" I bite down hard over my lower lip because, for the first time I can't seem to hold back the tears.

Mom touches her hand to my shoulder and looks into my eyes with a tenderness I had never seen before. "Really."

Ryder comes in and lands his arm around her shoulder. "I hate to stick a pin in the balloon, but can I ask what caused the change of heart?"

"You." She wraps her arms around him. "After Christmas, I spent a week just looking through your baby albums, and I couldn't stand the thought of losing my little boy. You know I won't live forever, and, in truth, I don't want to live a single day without my children. I certainly don't want my own stubbornness to be at the root of the cause. I want a real relationship with the two of you and with those you love the most."

It finally happened. There was a crack in the armor of my mother's soul, and it took almost losing us to really find her way back.

Baya and Bryson close in on our small circle.

Cole clears his throat. "I sort of need to do some apologizing myself." He nods over to Bryson. "First I owe you and Baya an apology for giving you such a hard time when you started going out." He turns to Ryder. "And I owe

289

you an apology for not being more understanding. I know what it's like having someone go after your sister. It can get pretty ugly fast."

"No hard feelings." Ryder shakes Cole's hand. "I'm sorry about the way I treated *you*. Keep your nose clean, be good to her, man."

A slow song filters through the air.

Ryder takes up my mother's hand. "Laney, do you mind?"

"Not at all." She practically shoos them toward the dance floor.

Cole picks up my hand and lands it over his lips. "How about it? You up for a spin?"

"With you?" I look into his electric green eyes, his dark hair slightly spiked over his head just the way I like it. "Anytime."

Cole leads us to the dance floor and does his best to hold me with his broken arm.

"Why didn't you call?" It all makes sense now why Baya left so suddenly. Note to self: Kill Baya for keeping this from me—and maybe Cole.

"Because." He closes his eyes a moment and looks achingly handsome in the process. It's pretty clear they couldn't beat the good looks out of him. "I didn't want to throw your game. I wanted you to fight—to win."

"Great news." It comes out despondent. "I did fight and win—for Melanie."

"I saw the whole thing. I'm really sorry, cupcake."

Something warms in my heart when he calls me that.

The crowd *ooh's*, and we look over to the center of the dance floor where everyone has shifted their attention and find Bryson on bended knee with a platinum sparkler in hand.

Baya screams and shouts *yes!* Before we know it, he's twirling her as they lose themselves in a liplock.

"Congratulations," I say to Cole. "Looks like you just gained a brother-in-law."

"Looks like." His dimples go on and off. "Bryson already feels like family. I'm glad he'll be the one with Baya in the end."

We head over and congratulate them as Laney and Ryder do the same.

"I can't believe this!" Laney squeaks with enthusiasm, which in and of itself is unLaney like. "It looks like we're all taken now." She pulls me in by the shoulder.

"We need to find someone for my moron of a brother." Bryson tweaks his brows.

Laney gives him a swat. "Holt's a great guy." Her eyes round out. "And you know who's a great girl? My sister."

"Dizzy Izzy?" Ryder teases.

"You're right." She smirks. "It'd never work out."

Another slow song starts in, and Cole nods me over to the dance floor.

"You almost ready to blow this joint?" His dimples twitch, and he gets a wicked look in his eye that I'm sort of digging. "Maybe celebrate our first Valentine's Day our way?"

"By all means." I wrap my arms around him as we sway to the music. "Maybe we can cuddle on the couch, and I can introduce you to a movie classic in the making."

"*When Harry met Sally*?" He looks hopeful, and I know for a fact he's not talking about the movie.

"I was thinking *Pitch Perfect*, but I'm betting we can reenact the one you wanted to watch."

"I like where your head is at."

Cole and I say goodbye to everyone and make our way out the door into the cool, crisp evening.

It's time to celebrate Valentine's Day our way.

And I cannot wait.

Cole

Roxy and I hardly make it to the apartment. She has her hands all over me at once, those crazy-soft lips pressed onto mine, and my hard-on knocks on my jeans just begging to come out and play.

"There's something I've been working on this week while you've been away." I block the door with my body, just losing myself in her hazel eyes. Roxy is a star from heaven that God, himself, molded to life in the shape of this beautiful woman standing before me.

"Oh?" She struggles to look over my shoulder as I let the door fall open behind me.

"Close your eyes. I want you to see it all at once."

That tiny dimple in the corner of her mouth goes off. Roxy closes her eyes and lets me guide her all the way to the kitchen. She takes every step with the utmost caution as if I'm about to lead her off the ledge of a building.

"I've got you, cupcake." I press a kiss onto her cheek, and she melts into me.

"You know my insides turn into water when you call me that."

"That's why I do it." I land another kiss just shy of her lips. "Plus, I mean it. You couldn't be sweeter."

"You keep saying that, and you're going to ruin my reputation."

"Give me an hour in the bedroom. I'll make sure it's trashed."

She slits an eye open and looks at me. "Just an hour?"

"Open."

Roxy takes in the sight and sucks in a lungful of air.

"What is this?" She takes in the newly painted kitchen, the row of new appliances that line the wall where the table once sat. "The walls! They're green with pink polka dots just like I wanted," she marvels. She covers her mouth when she sees the sign painted on the wall behind the new row of standing ovens. "*Sprinkles Cupcakes.*" She bows her head into her hands and sobs.

"Whoa." I hook my arm around her and bring her in close. "Tell me those are happy tears."

She nods, wiping her face down with the back of her hand. "No one has ever done anything so nice for me."

"Yeah, well, you deserve it." I point over to the counter where a very special gift I bought for her lies covered with a dishtowel.

"What's this?" She looks up at me from under her lashes.

"Why don't you do the honors and find out for yourself?"

Roxy plucks the towel off and sucks in a breath.

The mint green Kitchen Aid mixer stands strong and mighty, ready to churn whatever she might throw at it.

"Cole!" She lands her arms around me and plants a wet one right over my lips. "It's gorgeous."

"Is it the right color?"

"Pistachio, the exact color I wanted. You're a mind reader, you know that?"

"It's only one of my many superpowers." I grind my hips into hers. "Besides I've been looking for a promising business to invest in, and I thought what better place than yours."

"You bought all this with your own money?"

I swallow hard. "My dad left a little to Baya and me. I thought I should use my share wisely, and I think I did—I know I did."

"Cole." She shakes her head. "I don't know what to say. Thank you, for starters."

"Don't thank me. I wanted to do this. You deserve it. I've never seen anyone so driven, so passionate about what they do. Come on." I lead her toward the bedroom. "I've got one more surprise."

"I bet you do." She cups me over the crotch and gives a squeeze.

"Not quite that, but I like where you're going." I open the door to my old bedroom—her new office.

"Are you serious?" She gapes around the room.

The walls are painted the same cheery green as the kitchen with oversized dots bouncing around the room. A giant framed chalkboard sits on one side, reading *Roxy's To Do List...1. Kiss Cole Brighton.*

2. Make lots of cupcakes.

There's a white desk with a matching chair and a pale blue couch against the opposite wall for her to sit on while she trolls magazines for new ideas, or fucks me, whichever boosts her creativity best.

I give a lewd grin.

"You dirty dog." She gives my earlobe a soft bite, and I moan with approval. "I absolutely love it."

"Good, because I've got one more thing to show you."

"*No.*" Her features smooth out at the idea.

"Yes." I lead her back out to the hall, to the scoreboard where Bryson and I marked our conquests like two morons who didn't care about anyone else in the world but themselves. I pause and point up at my handiwork.

"Where did it go?" Roxy runs her hand over the smoothed drywall.

"I yanked it out and did my best to cover my tracks—put in new rounded corners, too. I may not get my deposit back, but I'm not too worried about it. I'm just glad it's gone. I like the new marks on the place." I nod over to the kitchen. "You make me a better person, Rox—move back in with me."

"Of course." She wraps her arms around my neck. "But now that my office is in your bedroom where are *you* going to sleep?" She purses her strawberry red lips, just begging me to take a bite.

"I was sort of hoping there was a vacancy in the spot next to you on *your* bed."

"I don't know, let me check with Sally." She glances down at her skintight dress. "You're in luck, we're feeling generous."

"Is that so?" I tilt into her. Roxy is hot as hell with her dark hair framing her pale skin. Those magenta highlights ignite around her like a flame. "Harry and I think maybe we should put together a little reunion."

"Rumor has it, you have a few boo boos that need kissing," she purrs.

"Lots and lots of boo boos." I dip a kiss over her lips. "You know what I like best about us, cupcake?"

"The fact our private parts have their own hit movie?"

"That and the fact neither one of us has to feel alone ever again." I assure her. "It's you and me against the world."

"You think we can take 'em?"

"I know we can."

I wish I could call my dad up and tell him I found the one. But I have a feeling he already knows. It wouldn't surprise me if he had a hand in landing me in an apartment with an oven to begin with. If I hadn't met Bryson, if Baya hadn't met Laney who introduced her to Roxy, it would have all ended a lot different, a lot more tragic as far as my dick and that scoreboard were concerned. The truth is, I needed Rox. And, in a strange way, it was because of my dad's tragic death I found her. I was never too hot on Whitney Briggs until he passed away. And after that I was so concerned with keeping his memory alive—*being* him—I made sure I landed in the very school he once attended. In a strange way, he led me right to my soul mate—right to the girl I plan on spending the rest of my life with.

Thanks Dad.

You came through for me one more time.

Roxy navigates me toward the bedroom. We tug at one another's clothes as we struggle to pull each other in deeper, tighter, harder, faster.

Roxy and I have what it takes to make it last. Love—a sense of humor—most of all, we have each other.

"You ready, big boy?" Roxy's eyes smolder into mine. "I think Sally is about to teach Harry a lesson or two."

I tilt my head to the side and bust out a grin that's been dying to explode over my face since I laid eyes on her this afternoon. "Make it hurt, sweetheart."

"Oh, I plan to." She takes a bite out of my ear, and I let out a roar.

Roxy plunges her tongue into my mouth, and we begin a wild ride that I predict will last all night—all year—decades, if we're careful.

Nothing beats Roxy and her sugar kisses.

Thank you for reading, **Sugar Kisses.** If you enjoyed this book, please consider leaving a review at your point of purchase.

*Look for **Whiskey Kisses** (3:AM Kisses Book 4) Holt and Izzy's story coming 2014.

Acknowledgments

To my readers who constantly rock my world—big tackle hug thank yous for being so positive and friendly. I'm so glad to have met those I have and look forward to meeting more of you in the future.

To Christina Kendler, I really couldn't do this without you. Thank you for being so generous with your time and so darn good at what you're doing!

To Rachel Tsoumbakos, how do I ever thank you for your amazing superpowers? You are a word warrior, girl! I'm so thankful you lend your time to my books.

To Sarah Freese, a million thank yous for carving out a space for me, time and time again. I can't express how valuable you are and how appreciative I am for you to put up with me and my constant harassment. Ready for another book?

And a big giant thank you to Regina Wamba and her gorgeous cover models—*rawr!* This cover is hawt. Great job all around!

And finally to Him who sits on the throne—each day I smile with peace in my heart because I am forgiven. I owe you every breath. Thank you.

About the Author

Addison Moore is a *New York Times*, *USA Today*, and *Wall Street Journal* bestselling author who writes contemporary and paranormal romance. Her work has been featured in *Cosmopolitan* Magazine. Previously she worked as a therapist on a locked psychiatric unit for nearly a decade. She resides on the West Coast with her husband, four wonderful children, and two dogs where she eats too much chocolate and stays up way too late. When she's not writing, she's reading.

Feel free to visit her at:

http://addisonmoorewrites.blogspot.com
Facebook: Addison Moore Author
Twitter: @AddisonMoore
Instagram: @authorAddisonMoore

CPSIA information can be obtained at www.ICGtesting.com
Printed in the USA
LVOW12s1952030216

473521LV00009B/772/P

9 781495 926532